Kaleidoscope

Gosnells Writers Circle

Also by Gosnells Writers Circle

Exposure (2015)
Lustre (2012)
Write Around the Clock (2009)
Pen Dance in Silver (2007)
Within the Circle (2005)
Gosnells Writers' Circle 21st Anniversay Edition! (2003)
Echoes in the Mind (2000)
Millenium Mix (2000)
Spirit of Life (1998)
Gosnells Writers Writing (1996)
Our Place — Gosnells and Beyond (1993)
Pot-pourri (1991)
Bicentennial Collection (1988)
Down Under — A Westward Look (1986)
Let's Entertain (1983)

First published 2017 by Gosnells Writers Circle
This edition published April 2018

Cover design by Jenny Lynch and Valerie Goodreid

ISBN 978-0-9758452-6-4

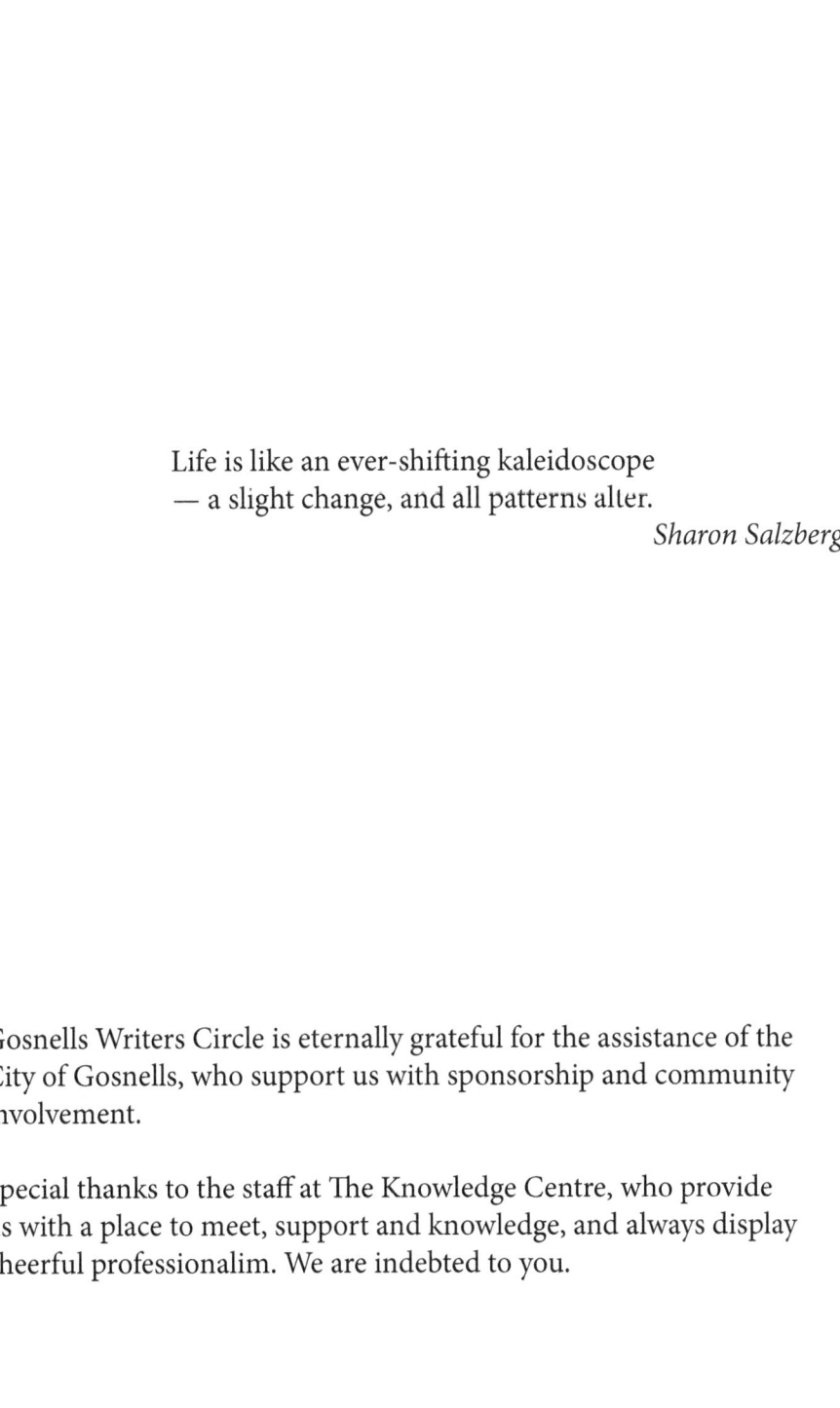

Life is like an ever-shifting kaleidoscope
— a slight change, and all patterns alter.

Sharon Salzberg

Gosnells Writers Circle is eternally grateful for the assistance of the City of Gosnells, who support us with sponsorship and community involvement.

Special thanks to the staff at The Knowledge Centre, who provide us with a place to meet, support and knowledge, and always display cheerful professionalim. We are indebted to you.

Contents

Sue Palmer

Kaleidoscope

I see the world through coloured glasses
sliding, fusing, blending,
Shapes and patterns come and go.
A twist of the tube can make it so.

Chips of glass in sequence dancing,
Hues of colours cool and warm.
Wondrous webs of tint and shade,
Harmonious colours changing form.

Multicoloured shards of brilliance,
Twirl before my eyes and spin.
I see the world though coloured glasses,
Like the windmill it turns again.

Mary Burke

The Balance Restored

"Shall we go out for lunch next Friday?" suggested Jane to her dear friend Celia. Needing to recover from their shopping expedition and the special exhibition at the Art Gallery, they were enjoying the comfortable seating and fresh coffee.

"OK. Friday at twelve thirty pm, Jane, at the usual city tavern," agreed Celia.

Both departed with hugs and waves, looking forward to their next meeting.

On the train journey home, Jane pondered on the day's events. What a bag of mixed emotions filled her mind.

Over twenty years, many holidays and outings had been shared with only minor problems arising. Was the friendship not based on honesty, consideration and common interests? Quite often Jane had tolerated theatre or film events which she didn't particularly want to attend, merely to accommodate her friend. Surely Celia had done likewise. Over the years both had exposed their faults directly or indirectly but were always able and willing to patch things up and remain friends.

Rather dramatically Jane wondered why the friendship had moved from the plain of tranquility to the eggshell plateau. Her conclusion was that it all came down to money. Neither of them was on the poverty line, while no one could call them "ladies who do lunch". This growing tendency to meanness on the part of Celia, as Jane saw it, was seriously damaging their friendship.

Excuses for Celia not paying seemed to be getting more creative by the week. If her friend had fallen on hard times for whatever reason, Jane was willing to support her, but so far Celia had offered no such explanation for her excessive thriftiness.

There was only one thing to do, thought Jane. She must bring up the subject and clear the air before it was too late.

Friday lunchtime arrived and this was D-day as far as Jane was concerned. Sipping on her Shiraz, she broached the subject in as kindly a manner as she could. Quite taken aback, Celia put her glass down from her trembling hand. For a moment, she couldn't get her words together.

Then she apologised.

"Actually, Jane, I am a bit short of money now," owned up Celia. "I might as well tell you the full story. We have always had such a wonderful friendship and I don't want to spoil it.

"It all started six months ago when my nephew Phillip called on me unexpectedly. Blasting out his sad predicament, I felt I had to help him. Without really thinking much about it, I gave him some cash and off he went. Soon he was visiting me more often and always for the same purpose.

"Apparently he has logged up huge gambling debts and was in danger of losing his job. Of course, I knew I couldn't go on forever doling out money but I couldn't bring myself to confront him until last month. I just made it clear that he must acknowledge his problem and get professional help. My supplying him with regular cash was not helping him but enabling him to keep going on his merry way. After this, he agreed to see a counselor and hasn't knocked on my door for two weeks. So, in a nutshell Jane, that is why I am low in funds."

After this explanation, Jane felt relieved for herself and her friend; but also sad and empty. "That was a terrible dilemma for you, Celia, and I really admire you for helping him," added Jane.

"What would you have done, Jane?" enquired Celia.

Jane grimaced. "Well it's always easy to solve problems when they're theoretical and not on your plate. I became so judgmental about you, Celia, and I must apologise," Jane confessed.

"Thank you for being so honest."

"I should have told you the full story earlier," Jane blurted out, "but I didn't want to lumber you with my problems."

For a minute there was silence, then both began speaking at once. "Great minds think alike," Jane quipped.

"I feel so good now that the grey clouds are dispersed and the balance of our friendship is restored.

"Let's give Phillip a ring."

Lynne Tatam

A Winter Solstice Tale

Pale yellow tendrils crept slowly through the stark, skeletal forms, tentative fingers that gently caressed the fresh dusting of snow, lightly covering the dark boughs. Frozen droplets of moisture formed exquisite shimmering diamonds that danced and sparkled in the sun's weak light, beauty reverberated all around me, bedazzling and bewitching. The sodden heavy earth was pungent with old leaves and rotting vegetation, blue wood smoke lazily drifted upwards, acrid and heavy it hung in the still air. In contrast the crisp, fresh scent of newly crushed pine needles assailed my senses giving an intoxicating head rush. Slowly I turned, absorbing all before me, my gaze drawn by the majestic landscape, muted tones of silver and white painted the distant hills which glistened as the dawns rays stealthily washed over them.

Tiny birds fluttered through the air, small feathered bundles of drab grey and brown twittering and chafing as they searched for tiny morsels to sustain them from the biting cold. Somewhere deep in the woods a single blackbird trilled with haunting sweetness, the notes rising and falling then gently fading away. Meandering through the snow hushed woods the frozen earth crunched audibly beneath my boots, I clapped my mittened hands together for warmth and exhaled loudly, creating warm clouds that instantly disappeared. Walking on briskly, defiantly ignoring the fine needles that pierced my face and stabbed at my lungs, ploughing on through the white blanket of snow I followed the noise of rushing water. For some strange reason I was infused with a feeling of excitement as I trotted down the path that lead to the swollen winter river, a frisson of electricity charged the air with something I could not define.

Metallic icy grey water bubbled and cackled as it cascaded maniacally over ancient Stone Age boulders. A large tree recently felled by one of the ferocious winter storms became a makeshift seat onto which yours truly gratefully perched. Delving into my wicker basket I retrieved the old red thermos flask and carefully poured a hot, life affirming cup of coffee. The first mouthful was pure heaven, decadently rich, sweet and milky. Quiet solitude wrapped itself around me as

4

the velvety mixture slid down my throat. Steam gently bathed my face and a wonderful warmth spread throughout my being, lifting my spirits—it was as if time stood still and I was the only one in existence. There was a local legend in these parts that dated back centuries telling of a magical white creature who sometimes mysteriously appeared on the day of the Winter Solstice, if you saw this mythical being your life would be forever blessed. No one could verify this story but neither could it be denied and so the legend lives on.

Suddenly, my reverie was interrupted by the snapping of branches, like a frightened rabbit I immediately froze. Pulse racing, heart pounding, carefully I turned around to view that which my eyes saw but my brain refused to register. Before me stood a huge white stag only a few feet away, his magnificent antlers wreathed in golden roses and head thrown back in pride, the regal pose told of his kingly bearing. Steadily the calm blue gaze locked with mine and lowering his enormous head he graciously acknowledged my presence. We stood for an eternity eyes locked, transfixed until he gave an almighty roar that reverberated throughout the woods and in a flurry of hooves he turned and was gone, disappearing as if he had never been. Had it been a dream or was it an illusion brought on by the cold? Curiosity took hold and I timidly ventured to where I had last seen the stag and there in the dank earth were hoof prints but even more amazingly sat a single perfect golden rose, as I reverently picked up the bloom its heady scent completely engulfed me.

Now, I do understand that many would think this to be a flight of fancy, a silly, impossible dream of a young and impressionable mind—however, this took place fifty years ago and I still have the exquisite flower. It blooms every Winter's Solstice day magically touching my world with its intoxicating perfume. As the legend foretold I am indeed blessed, as for one sacred day each year I have the golden rose, an eternal symbol of mid-summer in the darkness of mid-winter.

Christine Carmichael

A Birthday to Remember

Harriett Beckwith-Smith, the chairperson of the Monthly Wednesday Activity Group of the Swanly Ladies Club, along with her three committee persons of Marigold Summers, Hilda Montgomery and Agnas Copperwaithe-Inglis were finalising the details of the Club's forthcoming outing to Bunbury. The plans for the day encompassed a Devonshire Tea at a local café/boutique winery and a gourmet picnic-basket luncheon in a wildflower park on the outskirts of Pinjarra on the return journey to Perth. Harriet had engaged the services of the Parmelia Hilton Hotel to prepare the gourmet picnic baskets and all the accompaniments needed to make the luncheon "formal, but rustic" as per Harriett's instructions to the hotel.

Harriet was a person of impeccable taste in her dress and personal presentation and regarded herself as the Club's doyenne of all things etiquette. As chairperson of the Monthly Wednesday Activity Group, in Harriet's mind regarded as prestigious as the role of President of Club, she expected not only her committee members, but all the ladies of the Club to meet her high dress standards and to always conduct themselves in an upright and proper manner so as to project the image of grace and dignity when the group went on its monthly Wednesday outings.

The members, by and large, accepted Harriett's expected high standards, but with the forthcoming trip to Bunbury encompassing a picnic-basket luncheon in a wildflower park, it was felt by several members that perhaps the dress rules could be a little relaxed on this particular occasion. Harriett, despite a well-presented argument by the members, would not bend to this request and lower her expected standards. On the day of the outing the ladies duly complied, arriving for the coach trip in their best day attire complemented with hats and gloves.

Ironically, the day of the outing was the birthday of Agnas Copperwaithe-Inglis, but this fact Agnas had chosen not to share with her group.

At the cafe/boutique winery, prior to the morning tea, tastings were available, but very few of the group chose to indulge fearing Harriett's judgement of them as being "common". Instead, the ladies spent their time admiring the artwork of local artists which adorned the walls of the establishment. However, Agnas had other ideas of how to spend her time, choosing instead to consult the winery's wine list. Subsequently, hidden around the corner of the bar amongst the many other winery patrons Agnas indulged in quite a few tastings of a delicious raisin liqueur. In fact, Agnas was so taken with the drop that she purchased a bottle of the liqueur and four of the winery's souvenir glasses, all of which were quickly hidden in her large handbag before she took a seat next to Harriett as morning tea was being served.

An hour after leaving Bunbury, the group arrived at their luncheon destination, a beautiful bushland setting near Pinjarra. There were several picnic tables located together and the group quickly took a seat. After setting out the sumptuous picnic baskets, cutlery, crockery, tea and coffee supplies, the four committee members of the Monthly Wednesday Activity Group retreated to the last unoccupied picnic table which was slightly hidden away from the other tables by several bushes.

Harriett had decreed that there would be an hour and a half to enjoy the luncheon and the parks surrounds before the coach would depart on its return journey to Perth at precisely three pm. The coach driver had also been made specifically aware of Harriett's required schedule.

Having finished their luncheon, the ladies from the main picnic tables decided to take a stroll around the park to admire some of the beautiful wildflowers which were starting to bloom.

As the others departed, and without a second thought about what Harriett would think, Agnas produced the bottle of raisin liqueur and the four wine glasses. Initially, there was a look of horror on Harriett's face. However, when Agnas confided that it was her birthday, Harriett became a little more accepting of the gesture and the thought of the foursome drinking alcohol; even though Harriett confided that a drop of liquor never touched her lips before six pm on any other given day.

Agnas poured the liqueur and, perhaps due to her previous, substantial enjoyment of the liqueur earlier in the day, filled each glass to the top.

"I can't possibly drink that entire amount," exclaimed an indignant Harriett.

"Oh just get off your high horse for once and just enjoy the drink in the spirit it is intended," retorted Agnas who, on any other occasion, without the benefit of the courage afforded her by the day's earlier tipples, would never have dreamt of addressing Harriet in such a manner.

Shocked, Marigold and Hilda, not wanting the situation to degenerate any further, warmly encouraged Harriett to join in a toast to Agnas on her special day.

"After all, you do not have to drink the whole glass," chirped Hilda.

"Yes, alright, I will just have a sip," agreed Harriett.

Harriett then recalled that Agnas was a widow without any family and realised that sharing a drink with three friends would be the only thing Agnas would enjoy as a celebration of her birthday.

"Happy birthday, Agnas and we wish you many more birthdays to come," exclaimed Harriett, rising from her seat as she toasted Agnas.

"Thank you," said Agnas.

"This is really an excellent drop indeed," Marigold noted.

"Yes, I agree with you," said Hilda.

"I definitely concur with your comments, ladies," added Harriett who had obviously forgotten about just having a sip and whose glass was now nearly empty.

"Please do have a little more," invited Agnas who, without waiting for a response, filled Harriett's glass again and topped up the glasses of Marigold and Hilda.

The group had just emptied the bottle of raisin liqueur when they saw their coach driver coming through the bushes in the direction of their picnic table.

"Quickly, hide the bottle under the table and pretend we are just admiring the new glasses," ordered Harriett.

Marigold obligingly obeyed and the bottle was thrown under the table just in time before the coach driver was standing in front of them.

"It is well past three pm and the other ladies have been sitting on the coach for some time," said the driver.

"My apologies," replied Harriett as she, Marigold and Hilda rose from their seats and followed the driver to the waiting coach. As they departed, Agnas quickly gathered up the four wine glasses and carefully placed them into her handbag and hurriedly caught up to Harriett, Marigold and Hilda who, Agnas observed, seemed to be walking with some difficulty.

As the four ladies climbed the three stairs into the coach, each securing a firm grip on the access handrail, Harriett apologised to the waiting ladies, explaining that they had become engrossed in the beautiful wildflowers and had completely forgotten about the time.

There were four seats left at the rear of the coach where Harriett and her companions were soon seated. The door closed and the coach was on its way back to Perth along the South-West Highway.

"Best activity we have organised yet," murmured Harriett as her eyes closed and her head fell against the window of the coach tipping her hat from her head attached to which was her abundant hairpiece, both of which fell into Agnas' lap.

Looking at Marigold and Hilda who were gently snoring in the two back seats and Harriett whose head was now resting on her shoulder, Agnas chuckled silently and reflected on the day's outing, concluding that this birthday would definitely be a birthday worth remembering.

Sue Palmer

Sparkly Treasures

Sequins, diamantes, buttons and beads,
little treasures found in drawers.
Treats bought by Nanna
from crafty stores.

Lili loves to collect them all,
stored in pretty boxes.
Hidden away to be used one day
and a few kept in her pockets.

Out comes paper, scissors and card,
stickers, paint and glitter glue.
Pom poms and feathers
to name just a few.

The end result — a masterpiece,
to be admired by one and all.
Given a place of honour
upon my wall.

The Last Stop

As George parked his Ford Maverick, it said, "Nice choice, George. Lovely little town this!" George just nodded. Although Maverick had been talking a lot less lately, George had learned a long time ago that talking to your vehicle attracted strange looks.

He had parked his Ford Maverick four-wheel drive vehicle and the small popup camper in the side street beside the Commercial Hotel—the typical type of old two story hotel building found in nearly every small town in Australia.

This one had been recently and sympathetically renovated—retaining all the charm of yesteryear. George admired the bright red geraniums in half wine barrels dotted along the verandah as he pushed open the door into the main bar. After years of travelling alone, he knew that all the best information about a town could be found in the front bar of the local. Either from behind the bar, or from the local drinkers—all for the price of a beer.

"G'day love, give us a pint of draught will ya please?"

"No worries," obliged the lady behind the bar, sliding a bowl of peanuts towards him as she pulled the beer.

As there were only a couple of old men in the bar and they were in deep conversation, George chatted with Sylvia—whose name badge was pinned to her ample bosom. By the bottom of his glass, George knew where to camp for the night and how to get there. He'd been given directions to all the places of interest close by and invited back for tomorrow evening's "Roast Night".

"Local pork—with crackling—and all the trimmings," smiled Sylvia. "And I make the apple sauce myself."

"Well, I did have other plans, but I can't remember the last time I had a meal like that. Count me in—my plans can wait a day," George replied.

He climbed back into Maverick and headed for the Happy Wanderer Caravan Park. "Just two nights," he said, passing his payment to the young man behind the counter.

"Things are quiet here, mate," the young man said, introducing himself as Allan. "You can choose your own site. We've got a few permanents, and a couple of guys staying while they are doing some road work, but it's the wrong time of year for the tourist trade. What brings you out this way?"

"Marji and me wanted to travel all around Australia. We bought Maverick—I mean the Ford Maverick four-wheel drive—and the van brand new when I took early retirement. We had some wonderful trips. Then she...she... Well she died and we've continued on. Just me and Maverick. Now we've just about done it all. This last corner has always been just that bit out of the way—but we're here at last."

"Good for you, mate—I'm born and bred here. It's too quiet for most—but I love it. The wife 'n I have a holiday about this time every year. Go away to the city for three weeks. She visits her relies and shops to her hearts content, but we're both glad to come home again. Might not be going this year though."

"Why's that?" George enquired

"My brother usually travels up from his farm and looks after the park for the time we're away. His wife's not too good at the moment so he might not be able to come. We'll just wait and see. Nothing's booked, so what will be, will be." He closed his record book.

George parked Maverick and his van neatly close to the ablution block. Years of practice backing and parking up had made him a well-oiled machine.

Chock the wheels, unhook the van, pop the top, set down the step. Then pull out the awning and put out the little table and his one chair. He'd finally given away Marji's chair, to a young couple down on their luck, whose foldup chair had broken. He knew Marji would approve—and they were very grateful. For the final touch, he reached into a drawer and extracted a pink crocheted doyley and small pot of pink artificial flowers and placed them in the middle of the tiny indoors table.

"Makes it homey," Marj would say every time he'd suggested it took up space. And of course Marj was right. After thirty five years of marriage, he'd learned Marj was right about nearly everything. That's what made it so hard to go on alone. What was right? He wasn't sure he knew anymore.

He reached into the little cupboard and retrieved a can of baked beans. Easy dinner tonight. There'll be roast pork and veg tomorrow night. He went to sleep wondering if Sylvia would make apple sauce the way his Marji had done.

The following morning, he studied the map he'd picked up from Allan at the caravan park office. There were several places of interest, and he remembered the ones Sylvia had recommended. Stopping in town he called into the bakery and bought a fresh roll, then into the little shop next door where he bought some ham to fill the roll, and an apple. He'd already prepared his thermos flask.

Arriving at the picnic ground, he sat and enjoyed his lunch and a cup of tea.

He watched a young family doing the same. They all looked so happy. Well, he'd had his turn. Had his wonderful Marji. Had his own children. They had their own children now and were busy with their own lives. Now was their time.

George again studied the map and after one more stop, headed Maverick back to The Happy Wanderer. A shower and a shave and he was ready to go into town for that roast pork. The apple sauce was wonderful, as was the rest of the meal.

"Pity you don't do this every night," he said to Sylvia, passing her a spotlessly clean plate.

"Shepherd's pie tomorrow night, George. We have darts here and need dinner to finish early. It's very popular, do you play?"

"Not for years, but Marji and I used to play in a team at our local sportsman's club."

George then explained that Marji had died and he'd been travelling, most of the time ever since; and that he did have a house in the city where his grandson and partner were currently living whilst saving for a home of their own.

"I come and go, but prefer the country life now. I'm happy to sleep in the back bedroom when I'm there," he said.

After a little coaxing, George agreed to come the following evening for the shepherd's pie and to stay on for darts.

"Our plans can wait for another day, Maverick," he murmured as he turned into the caravan park later that night.

The next day, George had time to catch up on his washing and headed to the laundry room behind the ablution block. A hastily erected sign declared the washing machine "OUT OF ORDER".

"Do you mind if I have a look?" George asked Allan. "We had a similar one at home—and I fixed that a couple of times." By later that day George had not only fixed the washing machine, but fitted a hose to re-direct the grey water to the garden behind the laundry. Allan was so impressed, he located some tap fittings he'd purchased weeks before and offered to exchange free accommodation for assistance to change some washers and also have a look at the reticulation system.

"The place needs a bit of maintenance, while things are quiet, George. I could really do with a hand," Allan confided.

After a day of manual work, a good meal of shepherd's pie and several games of darts, George had the best night's sleep he could remember. Giving Maverick a quick wash the next day, George quietly told him, "Plans have been delayed, Maverick, but hang in there—next Monday should be the day." The next week passed easily, with George helping Allan around the park—even joining him and his wife for the odd meal, when not in at the Commercial. He'd become very fond of Sylvia's meals, and her relaxed company, and was sometimes torn between choices.

When Monday came, George locked up his van and headed Maverick out along a little used track deep into the bush. He marvelled at the size and beauty of the tall jarrah trees, edging further and further into the virgin forest, where the track had long since finished. He negotiated Maverick around fallen trees and rocky outcrops until he could go no further. The thick canopy above made it difficult to see the sky, with only odd shafts of sunshine able to penetrate the forest gloom.

"The time's come, Maverick. Remember the first time I decided to do this was the first time you ever talked to me. I couldn't go on without Marji, and I thought I would end it all...and go to be with her. You told me off, good and proper—just like Marji might have. You told me we would finish the travelling together—you and me—and then I could join Marji if I still wanted to. I think we've just about seen it all now, mate."

"I remember, George. I missed her just as much as you at first. The little pine trees she liked to hang to make me smell fresh. The dustpan and brush she bought to keep in the side door pocket, just for sweeping my mats. The pan pipe music she loved. And...she always smelled so nice."

Tears began to run down George's wrinkled cheeks. He thought of the hose and tape he had in the back of Maverick. He'd never be lonely again.

"You know, George, that Sylvia sure smells nice too. When you drove her to the hardware for more paint the other day, it was almost like old times. She has a nice voice too—sort of sing-song. So, are you going to let her down, George? You know when she bought that paint, she was hoping you'd be helping her finish the renovating. And young Allan? Nice lad, but really hasn't got much idea when it comes to fixing things, has he? He just needs a bit of guidance... of course what he really needs is a holiday. You could mind the place for a while if his brother doesn't come good. You know you could... And me, what about me? I'll be on the scrap heap for sure. No one will want an old fella like me. They might not find us for ages, all the way out here...

"Lets go home, George. It's roast pork tonight and Sylvia's expecting us."

Graham Bartley-Smith

Colourful Rides

My first ride was a blue and grey 1958 Holden.

Many of us may remember that time of freedom when we were away on a magic carpet ride.

Later as a necessity to handle rough roads, a dark green Series 1 Land Rover did good service and was replaced with a white short wheel-base Land Cruiser. This was bouncy and uncomfortable, and was quickly sold. Why I bought a yellow Renault Dauphine I can't recall. It certainly tested mechanical skills to the limit. Then it died.

So it was back to the reliable, easy to fix Land Rover. This one was an unusual ochre colour, probably a repaint. These were all pre-loved vehicles, as we refer to them. As roads improved a cream XW Falcon was added as a town car. When these two vehicles went to new owners, a maroon XC Falcon, a white Datsun 120Y, and a lime green EA Falcon passed through my hands.

Over the years the procession continued, to include an aqua Fiat Bambino, and a red and white Fiat Niki. These tiny cars were the answer to Germany's VW Beetle for the Italians. With their noisy 500 cc rear engine, cramped interior and slow speed, they were economical transport. So what if my head touched the roof and the pedals were too small for my size twelve clod-hoppers. The Bambino went to a restoration project and the Niki found a spot in a retirement yard. All the previous happened over many years.

One I almost forgot was a battle-ship grey Ford Prefect purchased in Auckland for a four-week holiday. Icy and mountainous roads tested its wandering steering and dubious brakes. When time ran out, and the car didn't sell, I put a note on the dash, "Help yourself". I had a plane to catch. Now to the present day there is a port wine Mitsubishi, a Kermit green thirty-four-year-old Suzuki Hatch, and a red Chery from China, crammed into the carport.

I haven't quite covered the full spectrum, but there's still a chance to achieve a kaleidoscope of endless colours. Does anyone know where I can get a purple Ford Mustang?

Knowing Me

You have spent time with me
And you know me;
You know all I do;
You know my thoughts;
You know my life
And where I am;
You know my words.
You watch over me
With your love.
You hold me in your soul.
From you I cannot hide.
You fill me with awe;
You drive the darkness
From my mind
And light the path
My soul can take.
From you I have no secrets.
I am yours for all time
And in my heart
You are mine.

Valerie Goodreid

Making a Masterpiece

He knelt on his cardboard padding, carefully putting the last touches on the final corner. He stretched his cramping fingers and rolled his aching shoulders, running his eye over the whole piece, checking for errors, parts that needed touching up, anything out of proportion or in need of changing. He picked up his brush and returned to work, outlining the final halo around the saint's head in delicate gold. He stood and stretched to let it dry before finishing the border, the last piece to be completed.

With the change in position came a sudden shift in perspective. For the first time he saw the mural as a whole. He had been focused on the intricate details, the work a series of brush strokes and tasks, jobs to be completed. He shivered, goose bumps rising on his skin. With a swelling warmth he realised he had created a work of true beauty. The central figure of the town's patron saint glowed with life, and the smaller pictures surrounding him, detailing incidents in the saint's life and the history of the town, were perfectly balanced in both colour and composition. He glanced around, looking to share the joy with someone, but the passers-by on the other side of the barricade moved on without a glance in his direction, intent on their own lives.

The glow sustained him as he finished the border, packed up his materials and left the square. He went to the council offices to report the project's completion, so they could arrange for the sealant to be poured to protect his mural.

On the train home, the emptiness overwhelmed him. The project had been his absolute focus for the past month and more. Day and night he had worked on it, preparing hundreds of sketches, trying different designs and ideas. The brief from the council had been flexible enough to allow him to express himself artistically. The freedom had been both inspiring and terrifying. Images had floated before his eyes, ideas for new sketches and improvements invading his mind at all hours of the day and night.

Once work began on the actual mural, he had arrived in the square at first light every day, compulsively drawn to continue his work. At first, the erection of the barricade and the initial stages of the drawing had attracted attention from the passing crowds, but interest had tapered off as he became part of the scenery—just a crazy man, kneeling on cardboard padding, painting pictures on the pavement.

The following day he watched as the sealant was poured to protect his work from foot traffic. The clear gloss coat enhanced the beauty of the image, making the lines sharper and the colours more vibrant, sealing in the image for eternity. He imagined his legacy living on. In future years would people point to his mural as a great work of art, speak his name in hushed tones of admiration?

With the sealant poured, the work was finished. He shopped on his way home, filling pantry and fridge that had been neglected as he worked. He cooked his evening meal for the first time in weeks, then collapsed into bed to sleep for fourteen hours.

Two days later he returned to the square to see again the beauty he had created. With the barricade removed, foot traffic now covered the entire square. His masterpiece was virtually invisible, covered by the tread of uncaring feet.

Genevieve Leslie

Truth

The truth is
I think about you
More than I should

The truth is
I'd like to see you
If I could

The truth is
I love you
More than words
Could ever say

The truth is
I'm waiting to see you
One fine
Momentous day

The truth is
My heart would pound
Like a Rock'n'Roller's
Drum
Whenever you were
Around

I haven't yet
Found someone,
Exactly like you

The truth is
I'm not sure
If I'd really
Want to

I picture the fields
Of lavender, at home
In the spring,
And I wonder
Do you still sing?

There's a uniqueness,
It's like gold and green
Something rare and
Unseen

You're smooth and rough
It's a combination
So sweet,
To touch

The truth is
There's no one
Like you-
I know this to be
True

18

Barbara Walton

Broken-Hearted in Broken Hill

The elderly woman sat in her recliner chair situated in a corner near the window of her retirement apartment in Broken Hill, New South Wales.

I do hope the air-conditioning service-contractor arrives here to check what's wrong with my air-conditioner soon. He said he'd be here before six pm and it is six thirty now. I cannot bear this oppressive heat for much longer. In my younger days, I'd have taken refuge in a cool bath, but even if I could climb in, I just know I wouldn't be able to clamber out again.

Then the elderly woman, Theresa by name but Tessa to one and all since she was about twelve years of age, felt her lips parting in a little smile as she imagined herself reclining in a bath when the young contractor arrived.

Oh my goodness, that would be so embarrassing because, as I no longer own a swimsuit, I would be unclothed. Accompanying those thoughts, a giggle had begun to coil upwards from Tessa's dry throat before it emerged softly into the stuffy room.

"Dear God, I need another chilled drink before I come to meet you in heaven before it's really my time." Uttering that sentence, the not-so-agile lady arose from her favourite chair and walked slowly over to the refrigerator and opened the two doors. She breathed in the icy-cold air and momentarily closed her eyes.

Sighing deeply, Tessa's hand hovered over the fancy bottle of expensive French champagne before reaching for the more pedestrian bottle of water which she'd only placed in there about an hour ago.

"Darn! It is only mildly cool, not cold at all, but the champagne is icy cold ... No! I will be strong and add a few ice-cubes to a large glass of this natural spring water. It's just as well I filled heaps of trays this morning," she found herself mumbling.

With a few of the small ice-cubes placed in a zip-lock bag (wrapped for comfort in a soft towel), Tessa returned to her recliner chair, turned on the telly, placed the icepack at the back of her neck and sipped from her glass.

She called it her "panacea"; so-named by her GP who had told her many times it was the best possible drink of which a woman of her age should copiously partake to keep herself cool in a heat-wave. She had almost begun to believe him—but not quite. Although water in any form—room-temperature or ice-cold—didn't produce in her the same exhilarating feeling as her beloved and quite irreplaceable bubbly, she had to grudgingly admit that imbibing plain-old-chilled H2O certainly enabled her body temperature to cool quite markedly.

After closing her rather tired eyes, imagining the drink she was sipping was indeed her drink of choice, she picked up the remote control gadget to switch the TV onto her favourite channel.

Eyes still closed and gradually withdrawing from her agitated state, Tessa became aware of her body responding to both the icy drink and the cooling neck-comforter—and of course to the early evening slight drop in temperature.

Sitting up straighter in her chair, Tessa thought, Goodness me... I am beginning to feel drowsy but I must not fall asleep in front of the TV—not when the technician could arrive at any given moment.

She slowly opened her eyes to focus on her immediate surroundings. The channel was snowy. In her distress, she had accidentally clicked onto a station that was closed for the evening.

Oh dear, just as well I am here alone right now. It would have been so embarrassing for me if anyone had witnessed Theresa O'Leary losing her usual composure.

Tessa, awake and in control, was almost her natural self again.

The travel show she so adored was screening a family oriented holiday film-clip involving a small boy about ten or eleven years of age. The lad appeared to be enjoying himself immensely—exhibiting such great joy from simply splashing and frolicking in the frothing shallows of the ocean.

I wish ... If only I could be there too, were her uppermost thoughts before delicious reflections of her past pushed their insistent ways forcefully into her hungry mind.

As if talking to herself, her thoughts seemed to chase each other.

What a happy sight for sore eyes. Just watching that young child cavorting in the shallows takes me back to South Beach in Fremantle.

If only my husband hadn't taken that Senior Executive offer way back in the sixties to come to work and live here in this hot and dusty inland New South Wales city...

And if only I'd stood my ground and stayed in my precious home-town of Fremantle...

But a wife didn't do that then. For all that's been said about the Swinging Sixties, the married women I knew weren't all that emancipated in those days really—more's the pity.

Pressing the TV remote's pause button, Tessa decided having twenty-first century technology was about the only plus about this place today. She brought her gaze back to the young boy who was now filling the screen, slowly taking in all details as she scanned the image closely.

His dark-clad lower half was half submerged in the gently frothing waves whilst his soaking wet upper body was clothed in a blue t-shirt which was a perfect match for the two blue kickboards he was clasping with both hands. This had been Tessa's first view as the video clip had begun to roll – and now she'd made it stationary so as to study it more closely.

For reasons she couldn't fathom at first, she felt compelled to keep her eyes glued to this stunning young boy staring out at her from the screen, beginning with his dear little face. Suddenly her heart seemed to be hammering in her throat, making it difficult for her to breathe properly. This youngster was the spitting image of her son, Sean, when they'd lived in Fremantle all those years ago.

Her eyes remained glued to the screen for what seemed an eternity. She felt like a person in a trance, staring sightlessly into space before refocusing on the screen.

"I simply cannot believe it! Look at those eyes screwed up just like Sean's when he'd found something outrageously funny; and that hair plastered in little strips to his forehead after a dip in the ocean. And just look at those so-cute Irish pixie-ears; all so like Sean's," those impassioned words spoken loudly to herself.

Tessa then sat perfectly still, her mind astonished at the uncanny likeness this "beach boy" had to her own dear beach-loving son. Her intense words continuing, "Nobody, but no one could ever have a cheeky smile and crooked teeth exactly like those of Sean, surely? His father, Patrick and I arranged for braces to be put on his teeth soon after we moved to Broken Hill. How our only child hated those braces— and us for a while too, for inflicting them upon him."

A knock on the door startled Tessa and the raised voice of retirement complex manager Tom Boyd called out to her that the technician Ray Browning had arrived. He added he had escorted him to her apartment door because of the lateness of the hour. She looked at the clock on the wall and was surprised that it was indeed well after seven pm. How quickly time had passed.

The two men came in through the door unlocked and opened by Tessa and, after she greeted them, they duly went about their business of "mending things". It turned out to be a minor problem after all and both men were soon bade goodbye from her apartment.

After locking the door behind the men, Tessa decided it was high time she organized herself an evening meal. Leaving the comfort of her chair, she walked into the kitchen area, now thinking about her current situation.

Since Patrick's death a couple of years before, and given that she felt quite able to do so, she'd continued living in the apartment they'd purchased a scant six months before he'd become terminally ill.

She could hear his strong voice echoing in her head, "Just because we now live in a retirees' apartment complex, Tessa, there is no need to lose our own autonomy. We don't have to be sheep blindly following others, but rather should just keep ourselves to ourselves as much as we possibly can."

Of course they'd become casual acquaintances with some of their neighbours but hadn't become close with any of them—Patrick had frowned upon that idea.

A handful of her close-by neighbours ate some or most of their meals in the complex's communal dining hall and lately Tessa sometimes accepted their invitations to join them - to be sociable and to not feel so lonely. She didn't like to admit it but times spent with other people were quite enjoyable.

Generally though, due to living with Patrick for such a long time, she now chose to spend most days by herself—reading, watching television, and reflecting on her past happier life on the west coast.

Her increasingly fragile mind re-lived the idyllic lifestyle she'd so enjoyed in her Fremantle days. Sometimes her thoughts became quite bitter when the resentment she'd felt when she moved to Broken Hill with Patrick and thoughts of the extremely reluctant Sean seemed to take prominence.

From when they first arrived in Broken Hill, Tessa had been greatly concerned about her son's deep-seated anger about leaving his friends, his school and his beloved South Beach behind. The indignity of his orthodontic braces and of course the mocking teasing he endured throughout the rest of his schooling in Broken Hill exacerbated her young son's problems.

Tessa's private and heartbroken thoughts seemed so often to be centred on their troubled son, Sean. She and Patrick had sought help from his school counsellors and from the psychologist to whom they had referred the sad and lonely youngster.

Devastatingly, she and Patrick had lost their only child—their beloved son Sean—just three years after they'd moved to NSW. He was just fifteen years of age.

The film clip of the beautiful boy frolicking in the ocean, seemingly without a care in the world, was a cruel reminder of what a happy lad Sean had been in his early childhood years.

This night, she allowed her mind to go back to when Sean, after enduring three years of relentless taunting from his co-students, obviously had felt that he could no longer endure his life, ending it at the bottom of a Broken Hill quarry.

Tessa clearly remembered her darling Sean's broken body when she and Patrick were called in to the morgue to identify him. From that day, their lives in Broken Hill were "broken" in more ways than one.

Her dinner on a lap-tray, she moved back to the living area of her apartment. Tessa's tear-filled gaze settled once more on the paused image on the screen. This boy could be a doppelganger for Sean. She brightened and spoke her thoughts out loud, "Tomorrow I'll phone the TV station and plead with them to make me a print of that smiling, water-soaked boy. I will call him Sean—because he IS Sean and I swear I will keep him near to me forevermore."

She realised that although she had never forgiven Patrick for burning all photographic and video memories of their son in anger after Sean's funeral, she could now banish those negative thoughts from her mind. She would finally have a photo of her beloved Sean to keep.

Tessa began to relax as she thought of the happiness her darling Sean would bring back to her life; she now knew that he would be with her for the rest of her days on this earth. She smiled hopefully at the image on her TV set as tears of happy expectation began to roll down her cheeks.

The uneaten meal lay on its tray on her lap.

Gone Fishing

Recently two fellows went off for a week's fishing along the beautiful WA coast. They beached a total of ten sharks including a tiger shark of two point five metres and a hammerhead even bigger.

In an interview they claimed to not have unduly harmed the sharks and that when they were released the sharks swam off strongly. Whilst photos were taken with them posing over their catch, the sharks were in shallows on the beach but their gills were always in the water.

The proud expressions and excitement was reminiscent of a previous sport angler—Zane Grey. This most prolific writer packed more into sixty-seven years than most in a dozen lifetimes. His novels and short stories have been adapted into 112 films, two television episodes, and a television series. An editor of many of Zane's short stories remarked, "Few men have resolved to earn a million and then remembered why they wanted it—Zane Grey remembered."

Fishing was his greatest passion—everything from using a hand line and a bent pin in the village pond, to battling the big beasts gave him immense satisfaction. Before WWII he spent a fortune exploring the Indian and Pacific Oceans around Australia and New Zealand. His catches were at the time, world records and remained so for many years. He was the first to land a game fish of over 1000 pounds weight. The Ocean City company made big game reels to his specification and bearing his name.

Zane was congratulated soundly for his achievements and the opening up of new game fishing sites. He truly was an adventurer who was praised for his efforts.

Unfortunately the similarity ends there. The two recent anglers were castigated unmercifully about their photos with the huge shark.

Seemingly not the thing to do today.

Even caring about the survival of the catch is not good enough for the "Green" people. Men must no longer take a pride in a very ancient pursuit. They don't need to fish for the family's survival so put away the tackle and take to the comfortable chair in front of the TV.

To enjoy a colourful day better find a real mystery package.

Emergency!

"Emergency. Which service do you want?"

The voice of the telephone operator was very businesslike, and it had a calming effect on Carol.

"Police, please."

"Police here. What is the problem?"

Carol took a deep breath. "I've caught a burglar, and I'm not sure if I have killed him!"

The police operator could hear the rising hysteria in her voice.

"What is your address, madam?"

"Twenty-seven Wright Avenue, Barnsley."

"Telephone number?"

"9450 6823."

"And your name, madam?"

"Carol Owens."

"We'll have a car there in about five minutes. Will you be all right for that length of time?"

Carol looked at the crumpled, bleeding figure on the floor. "Yes, I think I can cope," she said.

Putting the telephone piece down, Carol took another deep breath and contemplated the next step. Should she tie up the burglar, just in case she had not killed him? Or should she telephone her husband?

A groan from the floor made the decision easy. She grabbed a pair of pantyhose, managed to pull both hands behind the back of the prostrate figure, and quickly tied them together. Another pair of pantyhose tied his ankles. She used a third pair to connect the other two. With his feet and hands secured, Carol felt confident enough to leave the burglar and phone her husband at work, something she was discouraged from doing except in an emergency.

David was surprised to get the call. "Carol, what's wrong?"

"We had an intruder—a burglar—and I knocked him out. The police are on their way, but I had to let you know. I'm not sure what is going to happen."

"Do you want me to come home?" David said.

"I don't think so, at least, not just at the moment."

There was a knock at the front door, and Carol called out, "Just a moment," and then into the phone, "I must go. The police have just arrived. I'll phone you again when they have left." She put the phone down and walked to the front door.

When she opened it, one of the police officers introduced himself as "Detective Sergeant Phillips," and the policewoman with him as "Detective Constable Emery."

"Please, come in." Carol opened the door wide and the two officers walked in.

"Where is the problem, Mrs Owens?" D.S. Phillips seemed very friendly and casual.

"He's in the kitchen. I tied him up so I would feel safer."

"A wise precaution. Let's have a look at him."

The three of them walked along the passage to the kitchen, where the burglar was recovering consciousness. After checking his bonds were secure, D.S. Phillips suggested they moved to another room and sat down, so Carol could describe what had happened.

Carol indicated the front room and took a seat on the lounge. D.S. Phillips moved to an armchair, and D.C. Emery sat in another armchair, took out her notebook and looked expectantly at Carol.

"Tell us what happened." Her voice was warm and friendly

"I'd been to the library. When I got home I noticed the front door was not locked. I didn't think anything of it, just that my husband had come home for lunch, as he sometimes does. I put the library books on the coffee table there, and went on to the bedroom to leave my coat. I found that man looking through my jewellery box. When he heard me he turned and started to come towards me. I ran to the kitchen, thinking to find a weapon of some sort, and grabbed a saucepan. He came in after me and I threw the saucepan at his head. I used to play basketball and am a good shot. The saucepan hit him on his right temple and he fell. I grabbed another saucepan and this time I held on to it as I hit him. I should explain that my saucepans are cast-iron—strong and very heavy. He didn't move and that's why when I called triple zero, I said I didn't know if I had killed him!" Carol paused for breath.

"Then what happened?" asked D.S. Phillips.

"I grabbed the phone and called triple zero, then I tied him up, and then I telephoned my husband. He offered to come home, but I said I would phone him after I had talked to you. While I was talking to you arrived, and that's about it."

"Well, that seems quite clear, thank you Mrs Owens. I'll call for a wagon to

26

take our culprit away. First though, we had better check that he hadn't pocketed any of your possessions. Would you have a look to see if anything is missing, whilst we search your intruder?"

"Yes, of course." Carol stood and walked into her bedroom. She had a good look around, and checked the jewellery box very carefully, but everything looked to be in order.

When she went into the kitchen it was to find several items of jewellery on the kitchen bench, none of which she recognised, but she did recognise several small silver vesta cases.

"Those are my husband's. David collects vesta cases. Those were on display in the lounge. I didn't even notice they were missing. The display box is behind the door!"

"Is anything else missing?" asked D.C.Emery.

"Not that I can see," replied Carol.

"Well, it looks as if our culprit has been elsewhere this morning. He has been busy. We'll take him away, but I'll have to take the vesta cases with me also, as evidence. I'll give you a receipt for them, and they will be held in safe keeping, until after his trial. I wonder where the other items came from? We'll have to ask him when he recovers fully." D.S. Phillips was quite intrigued.

"I'm wondering how he got into the house," said Carol.

"We will have a good look round before we leave," said D.S.Phillips.

There was the sound of a siren in the distance, coming closer.

"That sounds like our reinforcements." D.S. Phillips moved towards the front door, and opened it just as the police wagon pulled up outside.

"He's in the kitchen, boys," he said. "Take him into custody, but you will have to get the duty surgeon to look at him. He got a good knock on the head, and needs cleaning up."

"O.K. Bill." and the two patrol officers walked through to the kitchen. They removed the pantyhose bonds, replacing them with handcuffs, and lifted the groggy burglar to his feet. With each holding an arm they escorted the burglar out to the wagon, placed him in the rear section, locked the door, and drove away.

D.S. Phillips and D.C. Emery then made a thorough check of the house, dusting several places for fingerprints, while Carol looked on with interest. There was no indication of forced entry, so the two officers assumed the intruder had somehow manipulated the lock, and made a note to have him searched for housebreaking implements, although nothing of the sort had been found on him when they had checked him over earlier.

"Are you sure you locked the door when you left to go to the library, Mrs Owens?"

"Yes. I checked it was locked. I always do."

A sudden thought came to D.S. Phillips. "How long have you lived in this house?"

"About seven months. Why?"

"Did you have the locks changed when you moved in?"

"No. I wanted to, but my husband said it was not necessary with the alarm system he had installed. Do you think the intruder had a key?"

"It would seem so. Another thing to be checked when we get back to the station. I'll have a good look at the keys he is carrying. It would be a good idea to have the locks changed even at this late date. You never know which previous residents may still have keys, but we can hope no others try to use them. Well, that is about all we need to do for now. Will you come into the station sometime this afternoon or tomorrow to make a formal statement?"

"I'll come in about ten am tomorrow, if that is all right?"

"Yes, that will be fine. I'll warn the duty officer to expect you." And with that the two detectives smiled at Carol, walked to their car and drove away.

When Carol phoned her husband it was to tell him the detectives had recommended having the locks changed. "I'll tell you the whole story when you get home this evening, in the meantime shall I call the locksmith, or will you?"

David was emphatic. "I will!"

Then she said "I hadn't killed him, but I think he will have a very nasty headache for a few days!"

Sioban Timmer

Hide or Rise ...

The sunlight couldn't reach her deep within her moonlit mood
          Her nerves were bare, her spirit stripped
                    Her soul left raw and nude.

Darkness seemed to bring some peace, in solitude respite
          So she slumbered in the shadow
                    Long days drifting into night.

Try as she might to hide away and the outside to ignore
          The universe came knocking
                    And wedged its foot inside her door.

Life picked her up and cradled her 'til the worst of it had passed
          Then firmly told her to get up —
                    And kicked her in the ass.

Choose to hide or choose to rise, time marches on each day
          Sometimes life will kick your ass
                    To help you on your way.

Forgotten World

Claire stifled another yawn as she waited patiently for her husband, Tony, to retrieve their suitcases from the overcrowded luggage carousel. She peered around at the milling throng of people, all pushing and shoving, trying to find their luggage and get on their way. She was exhausted and craved sleep.

Auckland International Airport was huge; a far cry from Claire's home town airport in Broome, Western Australia. Just two days ago Claire had stood on Cable Beach in Broome at sunset and in front of her parents and ten of her closest friends, she and Tony had married after a six month whirlwind romance.

It had been an intense six months. Tony, eager to impress her, had persistently sent flowers to her home and to her workplace. He phoned and messaged her at least ten times a day. He took her out to breakfasts, lunches and dinners and spent a lot of money wooing her, his gifts including a beautiful large pearl pendant from the Willie Creek Pearl farm. When he proposed just six weeks ago, kneeling on the sand at Cable Beach, presenting her with a pink Argyle diamond ring, she was ecstatic. How could she say no? No other boyfriend had ever treated her so wonderfully before.

Claire and her mother frantically organized the small wedding. It was just a casual affair, with a very short and sweet ceremony performed by a celebrant on the beach. This was followed by a dinner at Cable Beach Club Resort. Her parents paid for it all, including Claire's dress. They refused Tony's offer of payment assistance. He didn't protest.

Tony was not a Broome local. He was from Whanganui, New Zealand and had been living and working in Broome for a year. They'd met at Matso's Brewery one night when Claire was out for drinks after work with her colleagues. She thought he was very handsome, hilariously funny and was delighted when he asked for her number.

Tony told Claire that none of his family could afford to make it over for the wedding, so just a couple of his mates from work would be attending.

He'd told Claire to leave the honeymoon plans up to him. He had a surprise in store, he'd proudly said. The night before the wedding she had begged him for hints about where they were going.

"Is it somewhere exotic in Asia?" she had asked, dreaming of massages and cocktails by the pool.

"Not even close," he laughed. "I'm not telling you, except to say it's not Europe, UK or America, so stop asking."

"Well, just tell me one thing then. Is it on the Indian Ocean side or the Pacific?" she asked.

Tony just shrugged. "All I'm saying is it's not on the Indian Ocean side. Case closed." He turned and walked away.

Claire smiled to herself. It had to be Hawaii then or maybe Fiji. Either way, she would still need her bikinis, sundresses, shorts and sunscreen. She packed her suitcase accordingly.

The Virgin Airline flight from Broome to Perth was at three pm. The flight was only just over two and a half hours and Claire watched a movie and a TV show to pass the time. When they reached the Perth Domestic Airport, they collected their luggage. Claire still had no idea where they were going, so she pulled her suitcase behind her and simply followed Tony. He led her to the check in queue for Jetfly.

"We're still in the Domestic Airport," she said. "I guess we're off to Sydney or Melbourne for a connecting flight?"

"Yep," Tony replied. "We're going to Sydney first. Then, and only then, I'll tell you our surprise destination."

"Are we staying overnight in Sydney? Can you tell me that much?" Claire pleaded. She hated flying and hated hanging around airports as well.

"No," he answered. "We have a few hours stopover, that's all."

The flight to Sydney was horrible. The plane was full, the leg room was non-existent and the food was terrible. She couldn't understand why Tony hadn't booked Qantas or Virgin. She quizzed him about it.

"I got bargain airfares in the Jetfly sale last month." Tony explained. "Buy one ticket, partner flies free."

Claire winced. Where had the big spender from their pre-wedding days gone? She decided to grin and bear it. It wouldn't be long and she'd be in a tropical paradise, getting a nice suntan and sipping a mango daiquiri.

After half an hour at Sydney airport, racing from Domestic to International, Claire was finally told her honeymoon destination. Again, they were queued up in the Jetfly line. She looked up eagerly at the Departure board. Three Jetfly flights were departing in the next few hours. One was to Rarotonga in the Cook Islands, one to Nadi in Fiji and the last one, to Auckland in New Zealand.

31

"Have you guessed yet?" Tony quizzed her.

"Umm, I'm guessing Fiji." Claire beamed, her mind flashing forward to a much needed tropical escape for a week.

"Wrong," Tony declared. "You know how I said my folks couldn't make it to the wedding due to financial problems? Well, I'm taking you home to meet them instead."

"To Whanganui?" Claire looked aghast. She'd never been to New Zealand before. Sure, she wanted to go there some day. She even wanted to meet his parents, some day. But not on her honeymoon.

"Oh," was all she managed to say.

"You'll love them, trust me. And you'll love New Zealand." Tony squeezed her shoulder and kissed her on the cheek.

If the flight from Perth to Sydney was dreadful, the one from Sydney to Auckland was a nightmare. As it was now night time, after a meal and a couple of glasses of red wine, Tony put his earphones in to listen to music. Within five minutes he was fast asleep and slept the whole way to Auckland. Sleep, however, evaded Claire. In the seat in front of her was a young woman with a toddler, who kept crying and throwing tantrums. In the seat behind her was a young boy, around four or five years of age, who constantly kicked the back of her seat. At one stage she stood and glared at the boy. His mother was sound asleep. The boy just poked his tongue out at Claire. She sat down again and sighed. She glared at the sleeping Tony, envious of his ability to sleep through anything.

So here she was, finally standing in the Auckland Airport. She watched Tony effortlessly lift their two suitcases off the carousel and swiftly put them down on the tiled floor. He wheeled both of them over towards her. As he reached her, he looked concerned.

"You look knackered!" he exclaimed. "Didn't you sleep much on the plane?"

"I didn't sleep at all," Claire sulked. "I hope you're driving so I can get some rest. We are getting a hire car aren't we?" Claire suddenly had visions of a Greyhound bus.

"Of course we are," Tony replied. "Here's your case. I can't believe how light it is!"

"Well, I packed for a tropical holiday," she said. "I don't have any warm clothes at all. Maybe you should have told me where we were going." She sounded a bit miffed.

"Don't worry. My sister Jan is about your size. You can borrow some jackets from her."

Or you could buy me some, thought Claire to herself. She followed Tony through the airport, secretly longing for a nice hot flat white coffee and a bacon and egg sandwich. He seemed keen to get on the road though.

"Tony, where are you going?" she asked, pointing to the far end of the terminal. "The car hire companies are down there. See the signs? Hertz, Budget, Avis."

"Fret not, my pet," Tony said. "They're all rip off merchants. They charge like wounded bulls. I've got a bargain hire car from Zippy Rentals. As soon as we get outside near the taxi rank I just need to phone a mobile number and they will come and collect us to take us to the depot to get the car."

Claire's heart sank. Oh, Romeo, Romeo, where for art thou Romeo? she thought to herself. Tony was turning into a miser. Where had the generous suitor gone?

They waited in the blistery cold wind at the taxi rank for around fifteen minutes. Claire was so tired and was relieved when the old battered white Hi-Ace van appeared. She climbed in, ignoring the ripped seats, and buckled up. Tony loaded the suitcases into the van and joined Claire in the back seat. The driver, a large Maori man with a plethora of tattoos all over his arms and neck, turned to them from the front seat.

"Welcome to Auckland, Bro." He nodded at Tony and winked at Claire. "It's a ten minute drive to the depot. We've got your car ready and waiting." With that he revved the engine, indicated and pulled out into a steady lane of traffic leaving the airport.

Claire dared not close her eyes. She knew if she did, she'd fall asleep and she needed to sleep for at least a good eight hours. She glanced at the clock on the van's dashboard. Seven thirty am local time. No wonder she was hungry. She hated skipping breakfast. Hopefully once they got on the road they could stop at a café.

The driver had exited from the motorway and was driving through some sort of industrial area. He then pulled into a huge dodgy looking warehouse, where a dozen small white cars were lined up. The words "Zippy Rentals" in a hot pink colour adorned the sides of all of them. Claire winced. The cars looked old and a few had a dent or two. They were mostly small Hyundais and Claire hoped they were well maintained and roadworthy.

"Just come into the office, Bro, and fill out the paperwork. You are aware, I'm sure, we don't take credit card—only cash."

The driver led the way into a stale smelling office. Claire followed, screwed up her nose at the smell, dusted off an old plastic chair and sat down. Tony filled out the forms and handed over some New Zealand cash he had brought with him. They were handed a set of keys and pointed to the end car, a Hyundai Excel. Tony loaded their suitcases into the small boot as Claire climbed into the passenger seat. She looked around the car. As Tony got in, she said, "There's no GPS."

"No, that was an added extra," he said. "Apparently there's a map in the glove box though. We don't need a GPS anyway. I grew up here. I do know my way around my own country."

Much to Claire's relief, the car started effortlessly. They belted up and drove out. Claire keenly watched her surroundings, her stomach pangs telling her to keep an eye out for a café or takeaway food store.

"Tony," she murmured, "I'm starving. Can we grab some breakfast somewhere?"

"Of course." he replied cheerfully, "There's a McDonalds coming up in two kilometres. But we'll have to use the credit card from here on. I just gave all the cash I had to the car rental guy." He pointed to a huge billboard on the left. "It's not far away."

Claire hated cheap and nasty McDonald's food but at least it would be food in her grumbling stomach. She was starting to think that Tony had chosen a honeymoon at his parent's place just for the free accommodation.

Ten minutes later she was devouring a bacon and egg McMuffin and two hash browns, washing it down with a large, tasteless white coffee. Sated, she reclined her seat and quietly said, "Think I'll just shut my eyes for a short nap. Wake me if you want me to drive for a while."

Claire woke with a start. They were still on a motorway but obviously out in the country. She stared out of the car window at the lush, rolling green hills, all covered in little specks of white. As she looked closer, she realized they were sheep. Hundreds and hundreds of them.

"Wow!" she exclaimed, "I've never seen so many sheep in my life."

"Get used to it," Tony said. "They're everywhere down here. Sometimes they even get herded across the country roads and they always have right of way."

"How long was I asleep?" Claire queried.

"Oh, about four hours I think. We're coming up to a town called Taumarunui. Not exactly sure how far away it is but there's a sign up ahead."

As they approached the sign, Claire yawned. She was still exhausted. She didn't know if four hours was better or worse than no sleep at all.

"Look." She pointed to a sign. "Forgotten World Highway. That sounds interesting. Wonder what it is?"

"It's the really old highway that was used before all the motorways were built. Do you know, I've never actually been on it, even though I grew up in Whanganui, not far away? Grab the map from the glove box. Maybe we'll take a detour." Tony sounded excited.

Claire opened the glove box and retrieved an old, torn map. She unfolded it carefully and traced the motorway line from Auckland with her index finger.

"I'm guessing we're about here." She pointed to a spot on the map. "The Forgotten World Highway turn off is just outside Taumarunui. We should be there

34

fairly soon."

As Tony followed the signs pointing to the detour route he was about to take, Claire read some information on the back of the map.

"The Forgotten World Highway is only about 148 kilometres long, but there's around fifteen kilometres of unsealed gravel and the actual highway is full of winding roads. Hope I don't get car sick," she said. "Oh, and there's a note here, it's ranked by police as one of New Zealand's worst roads, with very slippery gravel near a place called Tangarakau Gorge. So drive carefully."

"I always do," Tony exclaimed as he left the motorway and steered the Hyundai down the beginning of the Forgotten World Highway.

After a while, Claire, sick of seeing sheep in the fields, fiddled with the radio.

"There are no FM stations at all out here," she said, switching the radio over to AM. After fiddling with the buttons and hearing lots of crackly static, she finally picked up some music.

"Oh, Tony, I love this old song," she said, as the song Smoke Gets in Your Eyes, sung by The Platters filled the car. "My grandparents used to waltz to this song every year on their anniversary." She hummed along as she looked down at the map. "There's a one-way tunnel coming up. It's called the Moki Tunnel and it's only 180 metres but make sure nothing is coming the other way," she told Tony. "It was built in 1935 and it is known locally as The Hobbit's Hole. I bet it's really eerie."

The old map proved to be a wealth of information. As the tunnel approached, Claire listened to the final section of the song. She briefly closed her eyes and could picture her wonderful grandparents at their fiftieth wedding anniversary party, gliding over the dance floor, her grandmother resplendent in her pastel pink outfit, her grandfather dashing in a navy pinstriped suit with a bowtie.

The tunnel certainly was dark and eerie. Thankfully, it wasn't very long and theirs was the only car travelling through it. The scenery on the other side was very picturesque, with beautiful trees, hills and of course sheep, sheep and more sheep. There were no other cars on the road at all. There were a few farmhouses in the distance but no people in the yards.

They drove slowly along the unsealed section of road. After a while a sign informed them they were about to enter the shire of Whangamomona, a town that had declared itself a republic in 1989. The sign mentioned the Whangamomona Hotel.

"Great," said Tony, "maybe we'll be able to get some lunch. I'm famished."

As they drove around a bend, a tiny town of just a few buildings came into view.

"I'm guessing the big old building ahead is the hotel," said Claire. "There are only a few other shops by the looks of things. But oh, my God. Look at the cars,

Tony. There are about eight of them and they all look really old. Like vintage cars from the fifties."

Tony absolutely loved cars, especially old ones. His face lit up as he pulled up and parked next to an old Cadillac.

"Wow, I think this is a fifty-one Cadillac," he shouted as he jumped out of the Hyundai and walked around the old car. "It's in superb condition. Look at this one too." He had moved to the next car. "I'm sure this is a fifty-seven Thunderbird and that one over there is a 1950 Buick Roadmaster. Oh, this is magic."

Tony was in his element. He certainly knew his cars. "This is like being in a car museum. It's awesome."

Claire was pleased to see him so happy. They looked up as a group of three young men and three young teenage girls came out of a shop door. They were laughing and talking but stopped when they saw Claire and Tony walking around the cars. They gave the couple a few funny looks and one of the young men walked over to take a closer look at the Hyundai. He stared at Tony but then just turned and joined the others as they walked into a second shop doorway. Claire looked up at the sign on the shop window, "Betty's Diner".

"Did you see how they were dressed, Tony?" she whispered. "Like kids from the 1950's."

The three girls had been dressed in full skirts, cashmere sweaters and bobby sox with flat pumps. Their hair had been pulled back into cute little ponytails, with very short fringes at the front. The young men had been dressed in tight black jeans, white fitted t-shirts and black leather jackets. Their hair had been short and slicked down with hair oil.

"Looks like the hotel is closed," Tony said. "Guess it's Betty's Diner or nothing." He led the way to the door of the diner and pushed it open. Claire followed.

Once inside, they both looked around. There were another twenty or so youngsters, all dressed in a similar fashion to the six who had just entered before them. They were mostly sitting in small groups in the padded vinyl booths. A few gathered around a jukebox, feeding coins into it. Music filled the room. The song "Rock Around the Clock" began and a young couple near the jukebox started dancing the jive.

Claire and Tony slid into an empty booth just inside the door. They were given a few more strange looks by the youngsters in the diner.

"Maybe we're gate crashing someon one's birthday," Claire whispered to Tony. "Maybe that's why they're all in fancy dress from the fifties?"

Before he had time to respond, a waitress flew out of the café doors from the kitchen, carrying a tray laden with milkshakes and burgers. She headed to a booth at the back of the room.

"Tony, look. She's on roller skates. Just like in American Graffiti. Oh, I loved that movie. And I loved Grease. And Happy Days. And I love all this old fifties music. This place is amazing," Claire said, as she started to sing along to "Sixteen Candles".

The roller skating waitress appeared, pad in hand. She pulled a pencil from her hair.

"What can I get you?" she asked.

"We haven't had time to read the menu yet," Tony replied. "But we'll start with some drinks. I'll have a Coke Zero thanks."

"And I'll have a Chai Latte please," Claire added.

The waitress looked from one to the other.

"A what and a what?" she sounded puzzled. "There." She pointed to the reverse side of the menu. "We've got Coca Cola, 7Up, Root Beer, Chocolate milkshake or coffee. That's it."

"In which case, I'll have a coffee thanks," murmured Claire.

"I'll try a Root Beer then," added Tony, "and while you're here, we'll just have a couple of those burgers we saw you take to the other table. They looked great. Thanks."

The waitress scribbled something down on her pad, spun around on her skates and glided back into the kitchen.

"I was half expecting her to say that she recommends the apple pie," Claire said. "They always say that in diners in the movies."

"Did you notice this menu doesn't have any prices on it?" Tony sounded a little concerned.

"Goodness me, Tony, how expensive can two burgers and two drinks be?"

"This place is weird though. They all keep staring at us. I'm getting a weird vibe that we are intruding or something." Tony stared back at the group they had seen out on the street. It was obvious they were being talked about. The girls in the group were speaking in hushed tones, staring and every now and then, one of them would giggle.

"Just ignore them," Claire said. "We'll just eat our lunch and get back on the road."

While they were waiting for their lunch, Claire took her mobile phone out of her handbag.

"I'm going to take some photos of this place. I love the fifties décor. The huge black and white checkered floor, the red vinyl booths and bar stools. Even those Betty Boop posters on the wall are very cute. I'll see if I can get a snap of the waitress on roller skates when she comes out again too."

Claire started clicking away on her mobile phone camera, taking photos of the diner décor, the jukebox, the groups of youngsters in their fifties costumes.

"I'm half expecting The Fonz or Richie Cunningham to walk in soon. Or Sandy and Danny from Grease. Feels like a movie set. I think I'll put a few of these photos on Facebook and Instagram. They look amazing."

After fiddling with her phone for a minute or two, she uttered, "Doesn't look like we have any 4G cover here. I'll go and ask if they have WiFi."

She walked up to the counter, where a young man dressed in white was scooping out ice-cream into little sundae dishes, alongside banana halves.

"Excuse me, do you have WiFi here?" she asked him politely.

"Why what?" He looked confused.

"WiFi. Wireless internet. For my phone." Claire held up her iPhone.

The young man scrunched up his eyes at the phone and frowned. He looked around the room which had grown quiet. All eyes were on Claire as she held up her iPhone in front of the young man.

"Umm," he stammered. "I'm not sure what you mean. There's a red telephone box on the far side of the hotel if you need to make a telephone call. The operator will assist you." He quickly grabbed the two banana splits he had made and rushed past Claire to deliver them to the occupants of the rear booth.

Claire wandered back to her seat in the booth.

The waitress reappeared with their drinks. As she put them down on the table, Claire asked her if Tony could take a photo of her and Claire for Facebook. She knew it was the right thing to do, asking permission first.

The waitress looked at Claire's phone. "What is that?" she asked. "And what is Facebook?"

Claire and Tony simply looked at each other.

"This is my mobile phone," Claire replied.

"Weird," was all that the waitress replied, and she turned and skated back to the kitchen.

"Tony, what's going on here?" Claire was feeling rather uneasy. "It's like we've stepped back into a time warp."

"I know, it's a bit strange," he replied. "Looks like these are our burgers coming now. Let's just eat up and go."

The waitress glided over, deposited the plates in front of Claire and Tony and disappeared as quietly as she had arrived.

The two of them must have been starving. They devoured the huge burgers in about three minutes flat. They finished their drinks and stood up to leave. Claire followed Tony to the counter where the young ice-cream man was cautiously watching them approach.

"Do we pay here?" Tony asked, pointing at the old cash register.

"Sure," the young man said. "That'll be a dollar seventy-five."

Tony and Claire exchanged glances.

"That can't be right," Tony exclaimed. "We had two burgers and two drinks. It must be more than that."

"Nup," the young man shook his head. "A dollar seventy-five."

Tony fished his wallet out of his back pocket. He handed over his Westpac Mastercard.

"Sorry, mate," Tony said, "I don't have any New Zealand cash."

The young man took the card and turned it over in his fingers. He looked from Tony to Claire, then back to the card.

"What is this?" he asked them.

"It's a Mastercard," said Tony. "You do take card, don't you?"

"A dollar seventy-five," was all the young man said, handing the card back and holding out his other hand.

"I told you, mate, I don't have any cash." Tony explained again.

Claire glanced behind her to find that everyone in the diner had gathered right behind them, including the waitress on roller skates. They were closing in on them, pushing Tony and Claire forwards, into the counter.

They all started shouting over and over, "A dollar seventy-five! A dollar seventy-five!" as they pushed and shoved Claire and Tony and pinned them against the counter. Claire was petrified. She struggled to breathe.

"Can you believe it, Claire? A dollar seventy-five." Tony seemed to be shouting at her.

She sat up and stared at him. "What?" she asked. "What's going on?"

She looked around, out of the car window. They had just pulled into the tiny town of Whangamomona and Tony was parking the car in front of the hotel.

"I said, can you believe it? Petrol here is a dollar seventy-five a litre." Tony exclaimed, pointing to a single petrol bowser.

Claire was confused. "Where are we?"

"We're finally here in Whangamomona. Fancy lunch at the old hotel? Think we can stretch the budget to a couple of burgers. Come on, sleepyhead. You've been asleep since just before we entered the Moki Tunnel."

Valmay Bartlett

About a Pantoum

You reap what you sow
a paradigm within a pantoum
a compass for life's journey
though destination's unknown

A paradigm within a pantoum
youths careless meander rooted
though destination's unknown
keeping a faith in the future

Youths careless meander rooted
teaching the value of nurture
keeping a faith in the future
tending the crop of a lifetime

Teaching the value of nurture
a compass for life's journey
tending the crop of a lifetime
you reap what you sow

Barbara Gurney

Mumma's Dying

To: aspencer275@gmail.com
Come home at once. Mumma's dying
Landra

"Hell!" Alex shoved the mouse across the desk and stormed off to the balcony. He leaned over the railing and watched people, three stories down, hurrying to their everyday. Landra only ever contacted him in an emergency. Ten months ago it had been Uncle Joe. Alex sent a sympathy card to his mother and six cards to six cousins.

He didn't want to go back to Italy. It wasn't his home. An East Perth, large two-bedroom unit, with a twice-weekly cleaning lady, and plenty of room for his Alpha Romeo, was home.

If he went back to Florence, back to the family home near the river Arno, he'd have to contend with Landra.

And Fia.

His brother, Landra, had never forgiven him for that July night, forty-four years ago.

Alex couldn't forgive Fia.

Fia's expressive face visited him in his dreams. She'd touch his cheek, kiss his nose and tell him she loved him, then turn into a raven and fly away. Just as she did in reality forty-three years ago.

His brother loved Fia since her family moved into their street. "I'm going to marry her," he told Alex every other week.

"Ah," said Alex, "is that so?"

Even at the age of fifteen Fia knew the boys couldn't resist child-bearing hips and painted lips.

41

When their father died, just after Alex turned eighteen, Mumma became ill. As the elder of the two sons, Landra, aged nineteen, was expected to take care of his mother. He worked part time in a bakery, earned little and, when he could convince Alex it was his turn to stay with Mumma, spent most of it at a tavern.

Alex studied accountancy and paraded his success. He offered the neighbours children countless rides in his new Fiat. Occasionally he'd invite Mumma and Landra for a trip to the country. Landra would have to squeeze into the back seat, his long legs uncomfortable in the small space.

Fia teased Landra. "When are you going to get a car?" She'd mock, "Alex has a car?"

Landra, hurt by the comparison, would look down at his unpolished shoes, and mumble about having to get back to Mumma.

Fia became besotted by Alex's attention. Their mid-week meals at the local tavern, the movies on Saturday night and the picnics by the river on Sundays, increased her infatuation.

However, when Alex worked away, Fia would switch her affection to Landra. She'd take her home-made panforte to his house and spend time with Mumma. Then, when Mumma had gone to bed, she'd flatter Landra; suggest he walk her home. On the way she'd flirt outrageously, convincing him to stop at a café where they'd linger over a glass or two of wine. Most times, before they reached her front door, she snuggled into him, her hands wandering around his torso. He trembled with her touch, and her passionate kisses made him want more.

So when Alex announced he and Fia were to be married, Landra threw his fork across the table and screamed at his brother, "You can't marry her." He grabbed Alex's shirt, pulled him to his feet, shoved him, clipped him over the back of his head, pushed him again, this time letting go as Alex tried to regain his balance. Alex stumbled, fell against the dresser. The crockery rattled, one ornament tumbled to the ground.

Alex put his hands out to defend himself against Landra's flapping hands. "Why not? She's my girlfriend. We're to marry in two months."

Landra threw a glass at Alex; it missed, and broke as it hit the wooden floor. Mumma yelled from her bedroom, "What's going on? Stop yelling, the two of you."

But Landra didn't stop cursing, yelling, hitting his brother until Alex stumbled out of the kitchen and into the street. He drove away and never came back.

Three days later, Fia packed a suitcase, met Alex at the airport and they whisked away for a new life in Australia. He'd convinced her they'd have a wonderful life in Perth. "I'll be making a fortune. We'll live in a huge house."

"By the beach," she demanded.

"Of course," he promised.

"And my own car?"

"We'll have everything you ever dreamed of."

Alex changed his name from Spagnoli to Spencer, lost his accent, but still couldn't find a job which paid enough to finance Fia's dreams. She wouldn't marry him until they had a home in Cottesloe. "With a marble staircase, wrought iron on the balcony, cupids at the entrance," she demanded. "And a sauna. I must have a sauna."

When he queried the need for yet another new dress, a different hairstyle, more cosmetics, she spat at him, slapped him, made him feel worthless.

After a particularly heated argument she said, "I should've married Lanny. At least he loved me."

"Go then," Alex said. "Go back to Italy. Marry Landra. I'm staying."

Once Fia left, his fortunes changed. He landed a job with a building company, enabling him to construct a home at a reduced price. Then he built another, and another. Sold them. Invested the profits. Watched his portfolio, and his bank account, grow.

Now he could afford that garish home by the ocean, but that was Fia's dream.

Alex read the email again. *Mumma's dying.*

For the last few years Mumma claimed to be holding on to the thin thread of life. One week she would be bed-ridden, planning her funeral, but, the next week she'd be wandering down the street to have breakfast with her cousin.

Mumma's dying.

At sixty-three years of age, Alex took early retirement. His doctor insisted. "You have to slow down. Spend some of your fortune. Go slow, Alex. Do nothing for a while."

His friend, Richard, said the same thing. "Go on holiday. Why don't you go home?"

Alex grunted, waved his hand at the scene outside the café window. "I am home. Italy ceased to be my home a long time ago."

"Don't be ridiculous. You're Italian. You can't change that. Even with a piece of paper."

"I don't think of myself as Italian."

"Well," said Richard, "I'm an Aussie now, but I reckon I wouldn't mind being laid to rest in the soggy soil of Scotland."

To: lfspagnoli@iinet.net

Is she really dying this time?

Alex
To: aspencer275@gmail.com
The doctor says it's inevitable. Get here without delay.
Landra

To: lfspagnoli@iinet.net
Flying in on the 28th. Will get a taxi. Booked at the Hilton. Will ring when I'm there.
    Alex

Mumma didn't die the week Alex arrived. Or the next.

Alex avoided Fia for five days, but couldn't avoid Landra.

"Still the same old Alex I see," said Landra, after he'd opened the door to Alex and spotted the hired Mercedes in the driveway. "Still with the airs and graces of the Mafia."

"And you're still sniping." Alex walked past Landra and headed for his mother's bedroom.

"Hello, son," said Mumma. "Come, give your poor old Mumma a hug."

Alex swung around, frowned at his brother then turned back to his mother seated in the sitting room. "Mumma?" He bent down and kissed her forehead, then grinned. "I thought you were dying."

Her chuckle turned into a racking cough. "Of course I'm dying. Aren't we all?"

"But," he glared at Landra, "I was told to come at once."

"Yes, yes. That new young doctor told everyone I was dying. My friends took up a collection for flowers. You know, Sophia, next door, she made five dozen sausage rolls." Mumma grinned. "We should have a party, for your return."

Alex sat beside his mother and took her hand. "It's good to see you, Mumma. I don't think you've changed."

"But you have, Alessandro. You look too old. Too worn. Has Australia not been good to you?"

"Ah," interrupted Landra. "The prodigal son returns."

"Leave us, Lanny," said Mumma. "I want to spend time with my son."

On the sixth day, Fia visited Mumma.

"Where have you been, Fia?" asked her mother-in-law.

Alex shoved back the chair and rose to leave.

"Say hello to Fia, son."

Fia kissed Mumma, tucked a blanket firmly around her knees. "Don't bother," Fia hissed to Alex.

"You two need to forgive and forget."

"Not likely," said Alex.

"And watch your manners. You're in my home now."

"I'll be back later." The slammed door expressed his feelings perfectly.

Alex left the Merc for the neighbour's grandchildren to gasp over and hurried away from his mother's home. Not for a minute did he think of it as *his* home, he'd separated Italy from that thought many years ago.

His hands clenched the inside of the pockets of his jeans. He stared at the cobblestones, his emotions mounting as he reached the corner. He'd hoped he and Landra could sort things out. Old squabbles, should be got over, he thought. Brothers should be mates, not combatants.

Left to the tavern, right to the lake. Either, or.

He sat on a wall under some trees, watched the ripples, followed the minute waves wriggle to shore and disappear into the pebbles.

Alex recalled a youthful day on the river. Two planks tied together, floating to the middle, Landra demanding he stay still, he not doing so. They had to swim back, but giggled like their female cousins as they walked home, arms draped across each other's shoulders.

Another time they'd borrowed a dingy and took fishing lines, bait, a stolen bottle of wine, and rowed to the other side. The wine bottle emptied, the fish stayed safe. Their trip back, with childish songs and lurid jokes, took two hours.

They had a headache to remember. Mumma had no sympathy.

Their companionship, their brotherly affection, disappeared when Fia made them compete for her affections.

She'd come between them from the first time she'd tipped her head, placed her hands on her hips and crooned, "You boys had better show me who's the better Spagnoli."

Alex knew he'd win her. He had "prospects". Fia liked prospects. It translated to status, parties, holidays. She could see a house with six bedrooms, bathrooms with golden taps and countless chandeliers.

Leaving his spot by the river, Alex retraced his steps, turned towards the tavern. He sat in a booth downing the first beer quickly, lingering over the second.

Busy scanning the menu, he didn't see Landra enter. Landra slid into the bench opposite his brother, waited until Alex looked up before he spoke, "You're here?"

"Why shouldn't I be?" said Alex.

"You told me often enough not to come here."

Alex motioned to the waiter. "You want a beer?" he asked Landra.

Landra drummed his fingers on the table as he glanced at his brother, then away, back again at Alex, frowning as he considered his reply. "We need to talk. There're things to say."

"You want a bloody beer, or not?"

The waiter hovered.

"Okay, yes."

"Two pints." Alex told the waiter. "And bring us some bread and cheese."

Alex drank the last of his beer and banged the glass down. Landra glared at Alex, but remained silent. His eyes almost disappeared under his frown.

"What is there you want to say?" asked Alex.

"Fia."

"What about Fia?"

"She's like a cat with its tail caught."

"Spitting and slapping? Yeah, I know all about that."

Landra sighed. "It's because you've turned up."

The waiter put their order on the table, acknowledged Landra, ignored Alex.

Alex picked up the cold beer, went to drink, but put it down again. "Mumma's dying. That's why I came. Nothing to do with your wife."

"I know that. I sent the bloody email, didn't I?"

Alex's breath oozed out, sucked back quickly. "You said there are things to say, and, while we're at it, there're a few things I want to ask. Things I should have checked up on years ago."

"What things? Checked what? You've been away. Living your life without a care. We've had to manage. Fia looked after Mumma so I could work. My wife had to look after our mother because you've been too busy with your houses by the frigging sea."

"Look here, you don't know ..."

"I know enough. Enough to know you could've eased our situation."

Alex held up his hands. "Okay, if that's what you believe. Maybe I'll let you live in ignorance. Let you think your wife is God's gift." He stuffed a piece of bread into his mouth, chewed rapidly, swilled beer around his full mouth. Pieces of soaked bread fell onto the table as he mumbled, "God knows that bitch doesn't know how to love anyone but herself."

Landra struck Alex's half-filled glass. It rolled across the table and into Alex's lap.

"Shit! You're a bloody fool, Lanny. Always were, always will be."

Landra stormed out of the tavern, cursing his brother, trying to work out how things had gone so wrong between them. He'd wanted to start again, be proper brothers again. He'd hoped this could have been the time to do so.

He remembered nights they'd sung themselves hoarse on the way home after a night at the tavern. The next morning they'd laughed at the other's hangover face, teased each other with Mumma's bacon and sausages and chuckled furtively while she scolded.

When Landra reached the street where Mumma's home stood next to his, Fia was waiting at Mumma's door. "Where've you been, Lanny? Why didn't you answer your mobile? I rang twice, left messages. I was just about to come looking for you. Although it wouldn't be hard to guess where you were."

"What's wrong?" Landra hurried past his wife, avoiding her slapping hands directed at his back. "What's happened? Is it Mumma?"

"Of course it's Mumma. She's taken another turn. I've rung the doctor, but he hasn't arrived yet."

Hurrying into his mother's bedroom, Landra stepped softly, knelt down beside the bed. "I'm here, Mumma."

"Is that you, Alex?"

Landra stood up, walked to the window. "No, it's not Alex, just me. Alex isn't here, Mumma. It's just me." *The one who is always here. The one who put his dreams on hold for you. Your first born.* He relented, walked back, hovered. "Just Lanny, Mumma."

Mumma reached out for his hand. "Lanny dear, talk to Alessandro. Tell him. He's your brother. Tell him. Work it out." She closed her eyes, concentrated on breathing.

The doctor came, left some more tablets, said there was nothing else to be done.

Fia made soup, lit the fire in Mumma's bedroom, kept the curtains closed, and told Landra not to include Alex.

"Mumma's dying. You can't expect Alex to stay away."

"For God's sake, Lanny, I don't want him in the house."

Landra stepped closer to Fia, grabbed her arm tightly. "This is not your house. It's Mumma's. Alex is always welcome here. Mumma wants him here." Landra stared into his wife's eyes, looking for compassion, seeing none. "He's come all this way. He has a right to be here."

"Right! What right has he got? He left ... remember."

"He's my brother. Maybe we've not been the best of brothers, but he's blood, you know, family. Family is what matters. Parents should care about their children." As he let go of her arm he noticed hatred flash across her face. "Children matter to most parents," he said softly.

Fia dropped more carrots into the soup and muttered under her breath, not wanting her husband to hear her curse the day she became involved with the Spagnolis.

Mumma's worse. Alex read the text and swore loudly.

He'd remained at the tavern after Landra had stormed out, ordered lasagna. Dabbing his jeans partially dry, he decided to book a room for the night, not risking the two mile drive to the Hilton.

He'd come back to Italy, because of Mumma, but he'd hoped to put the past behind and reconcile with Landra. After he'd arrived, it seemed impossible, but he still hoped. He no longer held any passion for Fia, deciding she was a devious, scheming female with no scruples. She proved this when she'd so quickly turned her manipulations onto Landra.

After asking the waiter to cancel his order, Alex hurried out of the tavern, hoping Mumma would survive once again.

He had never been able to make out what Fia saw in Landra. Any decent girl would've been pleased to marry a steady, hard-working man like his brother, but Fia wasn't decent. There had to be something; something she had planned. Landra was far too young and fit to anticipate an early death. While his callous sister-in-law would love to get her hands on his life insurance, even Fia wouldn't stoop to murder.

He walked unsteadily, but deliberately and reached his family home quickly.

"Lanny," Alex called, "how is she?" He stopped the door from banging, ignored Fia and entered the bedroom.

"She's stable. The doctor has been, given her something to sleep." His voice stumbled. "He said it won't be long."

"It doesn't seem possible," said Alex.

"I know," said Landra.

They watched the blanket rise and fall over their mother's chest, willing her to improve. Minutes past, then they both spoke at once.

"I'm sorry," said Landra.

"I'm ..." Alex nodded. "That's okay. The situation is difficult."

Landra moved towards the window. "See the street." Alex came and stood next to his brother. "Mumma owns that street. Every other day, for how many years I can't remember, she shuffles down there and has a meal with her cousin. Bella needs me, she'd say, thinking nothing of the pain in her own hips, nothing of the strain on her struggling lungs. The street won't be the same when she's gone."

Alex put his hand on his brother's shoulder. "We should be better brothers. Mumma would want that."

Landra hung his head, a tear leaked out. "I have to tell you something. Then you mightn't want to be my brother."

"What?" Alex shouted.

"Ssh, you'll wake her."

"What have you done?"

"It's not so much what I've done, but I guess you could say I'm an accessory after the fact."

"Good God, Lanny, don't tell me you're involved in a murder."

Landra shrugged, "It'd be easier to tell you if it was murder."

"What have you done?" Alex put his open hand gently on Landra's chest, held it there while he scrutinised his brother's face. One white hair in his shaggy eyebrows jiggled as Landra's sad eyes flicked back and forth. "Come, sit, tell me." Alex drew his brother to the couch that had been squeezed into Mumma's room.

"Now tell me, Lanny, what have you done?"

"I ... it's about Fia."

"Fia!"

"Hush. Mumma."

"Mumma won't wake. Tell me what that wife of yours has done."

"She ... when she left Perth; you. She came back here."

"Yeah, ran back to you." Alex felt angry with himself. It wasn't Landra's doing. "Go on."

"No, she didn't come straight to me. I heard from Bella that she'd returned. She worked at a night club for a month. They said she ... well, it doesn't matter what the rumours were." He paused, rubbed his hand over his arm as if he was cold. "She didn't come here. Not at first. Not until ..." Landra lowered his head, pulled at his ears as he fought with the emotion building in the back of his throat.

"What is it, Lanny? Come on, out with it."

"She came to me after ... after she found out she was pregnant. Three months gone." Landra's sobbing started. He didn't try to control the gasps of air, the liquid running from his eyes and nose. His head almost touched his knees as he rocked in despair.

Alex stood, walked over and watched Mumma's laboured breath. He thought of the thousands of dollars he'd sent for Mumma's care, how in the long run it hadn't helped. *Mumma's dying.* He forced thoughts of Fia away. *Mumma's dying.* He touched his mother's cheek, pushed the sheet away from her chin.

Fia's face, the feet that had stormed out of his house, the mouth that abused him, the eyes that taunted him, filled his memory. *Fia! Bloody Fia! Mumma's dying and Fia's laughing at us all.*

"I'm so sorry," said Landra. He stood beside Alex. "I wanted to believe it was mine. She said it was. Said the baby came early. And everyone spoke of a resemblance. But, I guess I knew ... I'm sorry, Alex."

"Why now?" Alex's fist clenched tightly. "Why tell me now?"

"Mumma knew. At least I'm sure she did. She never liked Fia. Hated her interference. I thought it was just Mumma." He placed his hand on Alex's shoulder. "You know Mumma. No one good enough for her wonderful sons." His hand dropped, he walked back to the couch, sat down. "Last week, when you and I were arguing, she cornered me, prodded me with her walking stick, told me to make it up to you."

"So I have a son." The thought whirled, whizzed, settled. "What's his name?"

"Paul. Paul Mario. For our father."

"Where is he?"

"In London. Fia encouraged him. I thought it best."

"Does he know?"

"No. I couldn't ..."

"Fia's played us all for fools."

"Not entirely," said Landra. "Fia was good to Mumma. Did her shopping, organised home help. It was Fia who offered to live next door. She looked after Mumma's finances, you know, paying the bills, keeping track of her money."

"Just a moment." Alex strode over to Landra. "I have to clarify the money situation. You say Fia handled it?"

"Yeah, Mumma found it too hard."

Alex sat, spat out his hatred, "That'd be the Fia I know." He looked closely at Landra. "Did you know I've been sending money for Mumma? Five hundred dollars a month. It was to make it easier for you."

"What? No way," said Landra. "There's been no money."

"Yes, plenty of it. I've been suspicious for some time. It was for Mumma. But I bet *your wife* spent it on herself. Had plenty of new clothes, did she?"

"She told me they were second-hand." Landra stared at his brother, trying to see a lie. "She told me ..." Alex shook his head. Landra shoulders dropped. "Bloody hell!"

"Mumma's dying, but it's still about Fia." said Alex.

"No," said Landra, "it won't be about her any more."

"You're right, we'll sort it out."

"Somehow," said Landra. "Somehow."

Accusations and counter-accusations went on for most of a long heart-wrenching night. The brothers were united in their anger over Fia's deception. After exhausting his emotions over Paul, Alex ranted about the money meant for Mumma's care, which Fia had misappropriated. Landra yelled himself hoarse, trying to make sense of it all. Fia's denials weakened with each passing hour.

The next morning, Landra pretended not to hear Fia's cursing as she forced the lid of her suitcase closed. As she emerged from their bedroom, he focused on the dregs of his coffee. His hand jerked when she slammed the door, but otherwise he remained motionless until he could no longer hear the clicking of her high heels.

Alex, Landro, and Paul walked the long alleyway together. Mumma had been laid to rest. Her life would be celebrated with a wake at Bella's home.

Frank Hawkins

The Coalition Forces

The bombing of the Twin Towers
In 2001, started the war on terror
President Saddam Hussein was blamed
Iraq was at war with America

U.S. President George Bush
U.K. Prime Minister Tony Blair
And Australia's P.M. John Howard
Gathered Coalition forces to go there

So the Coalition troops
Of the red, white and blue
Stars and stripes and Union Jacks
And the Southern Cross, too

Went over to pay back Iraq
U.S. army confronted troops of Saddam
As big guns lit the Baghdad sky
In the battle for Baghda.

Kuwait was the gateway
To the town of Umm Qasr
There were hit and run attacks
When the tanks rolled in to Basra

The Iraqis of Basra city
Caused several Coalition casualties
Including a U.K. soldier at Zubayr
In the effort to capture a terrorist regime

The power and water supplies
Were cut in the fighting
And the city's inhabitants
Faced a humanitarian crisis

Four thousand U.S. marines
Crossed the Euprates River
And Saddam Canal at Nasiriyah
With heavy resistance from militia

More heavy resistance in Nasiriyah
There more than thirty Iraqis
Were reported to be killed
After fighting throughout the city

British forces surrounded Basra
And they secured the airport
But faced small pockets of fighters
And the Fedayeen paramilitary force

The northern city of Mosul
And the oil capital of Kirkuk
Sustained aerial attacks and bombardment
The Northern Front bade them bad luck

West of Baghdad at Karbarla
In the battle for an important pass
United States troops were victorious
Securing a direct route to Baghdad at last

They also destroyed an Apache
Helicopter with sophisticated weaponry
That went down during the fighting
And clashes with Western Iraqis

Explosions rocked Baghdad
Targeting Saddam's Republican Guard
Barring southern approaches to the city
The Coalition troops hit them hard

In a wave of U.S. led
Air assaults, directed by S.A.S
And U.S. Special Forces
On B52's, Thunderbolts and Harrier jets

Life went on in the city
In the markets under smoke
From war action, offering vegetables
To civilians who coughed and choked

In the push for Baghdad
The United States army confronted
Saddam's best troops on the outskirts
In the bloodiest battle ever led

The Iraqi forces dug in
And prepared for the attack
As the city was ablaze
In waves of fierce air attacks

Fifteen hundred Sorties of Coalition pilots
Pounded Republican Guard positions
As the Coalition army were blocked
By Saddam's Medina Division

The red line for chemical weapons
Faced the convoys of hundreds of personnel carriers
Three lanes of Iraq's North-South highway was jamme,
Stretching fifty kilometres of tanks, howitzers and humvees

As seen by a marine pilot
When he returned to the *Abraham Lincoln*
The U.S. aircraft carrier in the Persian Gulf
Its navy divers defused mines to stop ships sinking

At the very front line of reconnaissance
Australia's Special Air Service Regiment
Controlling a highway near Baghdad
Interrupted an American journalist

The Pentagon confirmed thirty-six American deaths
Ten days into this terrorist war
Twenty-three British military had died for their country
With fifteen missing and five prisoners of war

U.S. officials said 4000 Iraqi
Prisoners of War were being held
Iraq provided no estimates of military casualties
But many thousands had fell

With the aid of allied air strikes
Kurdish guerrillas in Northern Iraq
Pushed towards the oil rich city of Kirkuk
As the Iraqi army faltered further back

The oil wells were sabotaged
Set ablaze by retreating Iraqi forces
The Coalition extinguished them with water cannons
And capped the wells for post war resources

In a day of dirty tactics
Four United States soldiers were killed
By a suicide bomber in central Iraq
President Saddam Hussein was thrilled

An Iraqi official later said
That 4000 Arab volunteers
Had arrived in Iraq for suicide attacks
Elevating the Coalition troops fears

Also with too many incidents
Of the allies friendly fire
It did not take Al-Qaida long
To put a "bird" on the wire

Saddam Hussein was eventually found in a cave
And subsequently he went to trial
But right up to the day he hanged
The former dictator was in denial

Judi Priest

The Birthday Treat

Pulling on her windbreaker and jamming her cap down over her short grey tufty hair, Lou stepped out the front door of her flat and slammed the door closed behind her with a bang. As the lock clicked to she gave a small sigh of satisfaction. It might just be a council flat but in the five years she had lived there it had become home to her. Not just somewhere to rest her head but a place where she felt safe and settled. It had taken her a while to get used to living in one place after so many years of moving around, but when you get older the cold gets into your bones and she had been glad to have a roof over her head for her old age and to be able to lock herself in at night, safe from the random dangers of the street.

The words "Las Vegas" picked out in sequins on her cap twinkled in the morning sunshine as she walked down the path pulling her shopping trundler behind her. Lou's fashion sense was eclectic and tended to the bright and glittery, with most of her wardrobe sourced from the local charity shops. This morning she had on a neon pink top teamed rather daringly with leopard print leggings. Out the front of the flats Stan, the caretaker, was mowing the lawns and Lou nodded a greeting as she drew level with him.

"Morning Lou," Stan bellowed over the roar of the mower, lifting one hand from the handle to give her a wave as she passed. Lou liked Stan, he was a friendly chap who treated her with an old-fashioned courtesy. Not everyone in the flats was as nice, some of them were a bit stuck up in Lou's opinion. Why they should think they were any better than her was a mystery. They were living in identical one-bedroom council flats and surviving on the old-age pension same as her. Lou gave a mental shrug. Never mind, she wasn't going to think about them today. Today was her birthday, her seventy-fifth birthday, and she was celebrating in style. Lou trotted along briskly, the shopping trundler squeaking and bumping along behind her, a smile on her face as she contemplated the special birthday morning tea she had planned. A proper fancy coffee and a piece of cake, or maybe a slice, she hadn't made up her mind yet.

Reaching the shops Lou slowed her pace so she could window shop as she passed. When she reached the Red Cross shop in the middle of the block she stopped, peering through the window to see what new treasures had arrived in the past week. That was the thing with the charity shops, you never knew from one day to the next what they might have. Every day brought something new and interesting.

"Hello, Lou. How're you going?" the young woman at the counter looked up and greeted her brightly as she came through the door.

"Good morning, love!"

"Leave your trolley here while you have a look round, if you like." The girl waved at the space at the end of the counter.

"Thanks, that would be great."

Lou parked her trolley and headed off to scan the shelves. She wandered happily through the china and glassware, picking up a china cat and studying it closely before replacing it on the shelf. In the clothing department she picked out a coat, holding it against her and stroking the soft fabric. She checked the label—ten dollars! Daylight robbery!—before replacing it on the rack. Oh well, winter was months away and if she waited a bit they would probably reduce the price. As she made her way back towards the front of the shop she spied, low down on a display stand, a pair of pale green sandals with large, glittering stones across the top.

Two dollars! A bargain! And the right size!

Lou levered one sneaker off with her other foot and bending down, pulled on one of the sandals, admiring the way the stones sparkled as she turned her foot one way then the other. A bit tight but she could adjust the straps at the back and they would be perfect. With a triumphant grin she clutched the sandals to her chest and headed to the counter.

"What pretty sandals! And a bargain price—good spotting!"

The young woman smiled at Lou who was balancing on one foot as she put her sneaker back on. With a whoof of breath she straightened up and reaching into her trolley she rummaged round for her purse.

"Thanks, love."

Lou pushed two dollars across the counter and a few minutes later she was back outside on the footpath and heading purposefully for the café, the pretty green sandals safely stowed in her trusty trolley.

At the café Lou ordered a cappuccino and a slice of chocolate mud cake, thick with icing and covered in curls of shaved chocolate. She sat at a table near the door, drinking her coffee and eating her cake slowly, savouring each bite as she watched people coming and going from the shopping mall next door. There were families with laughing children, young couples holding hands (and some older couples which made her smile) but mostly there were lots of middle aged women, burdened by bags full of shopping. Lou wondered how much they had spent, those women, and whether they would be as pleased with their purchases as she was with her green sandals. As she watched, one of the women shoppers came into the café and took a seat at the next table, piling her parcels on the empty chair beside her. Lou gave her an expansive smile and nodded towards the pile of shopping bags,

"You've had a busy morning!"

But the woman didn't reply, instead turning away and pulling out her phone, stabbing at the keyboard with a long red painted fingernail. As Lou watched the woman drank her coffee—A long black and no cake for her, no wonder she was skinny and mean!—and then pulled out a lipstick and compact and freshened her make up.

Meeting somebody, Lou thought.

Somebody worth making an effort for, by the looks of things.

Lou took three sachets of sugar from the sugar bowl and sliding them across the table she palmed them before slipping them into her pocket. She didn't take sugar in her coffee but she could have and she had come to the logical conclusion that since the price included sugar she had paid for it and was entitled to it. Lou liked to get her money's worth. Whether it harked back to past hardships wasn't clear but the small steady purloining of sugar sachets made her feel safe somehow, like a squirrel saving nuts against the prospect of winter. The stashing of the sugar was accomplished unobtrusively but when Lou looked round the woman was watching her, a frown creasing her face and her freshly glossy lips set in a hard, red line.

"Well, really!"

With a snort of disapproval, the woman gathered up her bags and swept out the door and was gone. Lou blinked and swallowed, shuffling the illicit sugar packets in her pocket. She wasn't going to let that painted Jezebel make her feel bad. She had paid for sugar and she was entitled to sugar. And it was her birthday, her seventy-fifth birthday. She wasn't going to let anyone make her feel bad on her special day. She drank the last of her coffee but it was barely warm now and the pleasure had gone out of it.

Lou gathered up her trolley and her jacket and bent down to re-tie her shoelace which had come undone—probably loosened when she was trying on the sandal in the Red Cross shop. As she straightened up she saw a slip of paper under the next table and she reached over to pick it up, turning it over to read the printed words on the other side. It was a voucher—a voucher for a pedicure. The woman with the shopping must have dropped it when she scrabbled in her bag for her lipstick. Lou looked to where she had last seen the woman. Well, she was gone now. Gone and good riddance to her with her red lips and her disapproving glare. A thought was forming in Lou's mind. She read the voucher again. It was for a pedicure at the Pretty Nail Spa Salon in the mall next door. Lou had never had a pedicure; she'd never had a manicure either come to that. Well, today was her birthday and she was treating herself and she had a new pair of pretty, pale green sandals with sparkly stones. Lou stuffed the voucher into her pocket along with the sugar sachets and set off to the mall. With luck she could have her pedicure and still be home in time for lunch.

Alligator Allegations

I thought I'd try something else. How would you like to lay all day and all night at the bottom of a muddy swamp with only your eyeball sticking out of the water? Occasionally a stupid dog or some such beast would be dumb enough to swim too close so it would be my natural duty to eat it; the remainder of my diet was any rotten corpse that happened to float by. The other thing that really annoyed me was little white balls splashing into my pool, the bottom was covered with them, and if one happened to hit you it hurt.

I was doing my job, lurking at the edge of my swamp when just such a ball whacked me right on my snout. Boy! Was I mad. I threshed my tail (that's the terminology we crocodilians use for waving it about), opened my jaws and charged at this tall, skinny beast who had hit the ball. He backed off pretty damn quickly I can tell you, but I had my cold blood up and pumping so I pursued him. I didn't really fancy eating him as I'd just demolished a bellyful of rotted snake, anyway! He looked paler than some of the oldest carrion I'd ever eaten so, after I had bailed him up against a tree I didn't know what to do next, I spoke to him in my loudest hissing roar.

"What the hell do you think you're doing? Those bloody white things are dangerous."

"S's'sorry, " he stuttered, "I didn't really want to lose my ball in the water, it was the last one I had and losing them gets expensive."

"Expensive eh!" A light flashed on in my brain, "How expensive? Expensive as a T bone steak?"

"You could buy a bucket of T bones if you had enough balls to sell."

"Well the bottom of the swamp is covered with them, why don't you recover some?"

"Because the swamp is full of vicious alligators."

"Yes! I forgot about them—us. Buuut! What if I recovered them and you sold them and split fifty-fifty, my half in steaks?"

My something else had appeared and that is why I am the fattest alligator in the swamp and a fully paid up member of the best golf club in the city.

Dianne Taylor

Static Caravans

As we drove into Ladran Bay Caravan Park on the south west of England, the view was beautiful, with cliffs overhanging the bay. It reminded us of Kalbarri, north of Perth. The comparison finished there, as this was a collection of static caravans, set out in orderly lines like soldiers marching down the hill. They overlooked the beautiful bay beyond the cliffs. We had booked one of these caravans, recommended by Rick's sister.

As this was our first experience of static caravans, we were impressed with the quality of the vans. Each van was self-contained, fitted out with a bathroom, kitchen, bedroom and lounge area. The kitchen was clean and fully stocked with crockery, cutlery and cooking utensils. All we had to supply were food and tea towels. The bedroom included linen; we only had to supply towels. It was ideal for us, on holiday from overseas. There was the advantage of cooking our own meals, a relief after eating hotel food. It was also cheaper to buy food, then cook it. One of our favourite dishes was salmon, cheap and plentiful in England.

While exploring our park, we found a small area for people with their own vans, separate from the static caravans. We were surprised to find there were no barbeques, camp kitchens, or other facilities that were present in Australian caravan parks—I suppose we could blame English weather. There were some small shops/takeaways and a bar/restaurant (very expensive) with water views. As for the beach, it was a real disappointment. There was limited access via a boat ramp, and a small stone beach with a few deck chairs and small boats in the bay—not really suitable for swimming.

The walk up to the cliffs was steep and challenging, but the view at the top was spectacular. There was also a walk trail in the other direction, which was easier to manage. We saw quite a few people standing at the top of the cliff, or walking on the easier trail. We stayed for three days, giving ourselves the chance to explore the local area by car. The weather was also beautiful, fine and warm. I even got a bit sunburnt.

After leaving Ladran Bay, we headed for Wales. Searching for accommodation, we found a place on the West Coast, which had several static caravans available. After our previous experience, we thought another static caravan would be ideal. The caravan park was close to a small town, Haverford West. We found the supermarket, bought some supplies, then headed out to our caravan park. As we drove in, we noticed several static caravans that looked very comfortable and well maintained. Of course, we didn't know that these vans were privately owned. Once we registered and paid for our stay, the grumpy old woman led us to our van. We drove past the fine vans, around the corner and downhill. At the bottom of the park, there was a terrible old van that must have been around forty years old. You guessed it, that was our van. What a shock!

Coming from Ladran Bay, we couldn't believe the difference. From the living room, we could talk to the cows in the nearby field—very rustic. We decided to make the best of it; we had paid for four days. On exploring our temporary home, we found the gas hot water system for the kitchen was a unit next to the cupboards, which constantly made a popping sound. There was a gas bottle outside, under the kitchen window, which didn't seem to be very full. We felt pretty insecure, we could be blown up at any minute. Unfortunately, the hot water and room heater were all gas, and the weather had turned cold and wet. We took our mucky shoes off at the door and went to bed fully clothed.

On the first evening we tried to check our emails, only to discover that this park had no internet.

With advice from one of our friendly neighbours, we found the local library the next day which offered free WiFi, and a friendly librarian. While exploring the town, we found other places with free WiFi, such as the pub and a coffee shop.

Just as we finished in town, it started to rain, accompanied by a cold wind. We returned to our car, sloshing our way up a steep hill in the rain. After surviving the cold miserable weather and the dreadful old van for two days, we decided to leave early, and head for warmer weather.

Trevor Smith

A Big Enough Lie

We had everything. Many adults regarded us as spoilt brats and looking back on those kindergarten years I have to agree with that opinion. Then after junior school we were enrolled at the best private school in the town.

From our first day at this exclusive seat of learning my buddy, Greg, set about making a name for himself. I watched amazed when he brazenly demanded to see the other kids lunch and after examination of their packages he helped himself to whatever he fancied. That was just the beginning. He set about openly defying all school regulations and seemed to take delight in the punishments that were awarded. In those times a severe caning was often administered but Greg would simply brag about how many he had received. This open defiance of rules brought him to the attention of the entire school. He was encouraged by rebel seniors who invited him to join them in some of their rebellious pranks.

I was mocked by Greg and his new cronies when I refused to join them in one of their more daring escapades. Thereafter I was never considered part of the gang. Tobacco in the far corner of the playground was never carefully hidden but when they got onto other stuff they did become a bit more discreet. Those recreational drugs and alcohol became a major part of life for him and his gang. Obscene graffiti was plastered over many of the walls visible to the passing public, light fittings and other fixtures were smashed, windows were broken and on a couple of occasions cash was stolen from the secretary's office.

This unruly behaviour spread into the surrounding town areas and although perpetrators were never caught and convicted it was obvious to us at the school that Greg and his gang were the guilty parties. Greg regarded study as completely unnecessary and he took pleasure in upsetting teachers by never completing assignments. Despite his careless attitude he always ended each term with the top marks in all subjects. The final public examinations he passed with honours and entrance to our local University was automatic. Two years at Uni and he simply sailed through each subject despite being the "main man" in a group of unruly hoodlums. These hoods went completely wild and their misdemeanours became a long list of unsolved crime. The police also had their suspicions and Greg eventually was taken for interrogation. He received such a stern warning that he decided to leave town. His academic record was so good that he was immediately accepted at a university in our neighbouring state.

Many years later whilst sitting in the waiting room at my dentist I was scanning the only available magazine—*Woman's Own*. Suddenly staring up at me from the centre page was a handsome, smiling Greg. Gazing rapturously up at him in the photograph was a beautiful young miss. Below the glossy full page photograph was the note: "Vanessa, star of television and a leading light on the catwalk, has become engaged to Gregory McKenzie. Her father, Sir Reginald Donovan, remarked how the whole family was delighted to welcome such an accomplished young man into their midst."

I could not believe it! "Delighted—Accomplished" and attributed to our respected and beloved State Governor. Where could I find the facts behind such a statement? Google. Then there it was on my computer: "Gregory McKenzie—leader of the team engaged in analysis of the extensive archaeological diggings in Northern Italy ..." on and on about this particular venture then about the man: "... a brilliant young man from a respected background who was a leading light in his group at university. His determination and devotion to study resulted in the youngest ever recipient of a PhD History."

I knew he was supposed to be studying history but how good he became was news to me. Now there was no way I could doubt his ability—he had to be a complete genius in history because the printed word about his exemplary background proved he had very successfully been able to "un-write" the true facts.

"If you tell a big enough lie, and tell it frequently enough, it will be believed." So said Adolf Hitler and if he had been victorious would the true facts of the holocaust be recorded in history? Reactionaries would like to rewrite history to deny that it ever happened. Another dictatorial despot who has followed a similar path is Robert Gabriel Mugabe. The unwritten history of his rise to power is very different from the facts as he has directed that they be recorded. The 20,000 Matabele murdered by his Chinese trained 5th Brigade will remain unwritten in the history of Zimbabwe as long as Mugabe lives.

Only Five Days

"What have you got for me, Carole? I need a story ready for next week. Any ideas? You're our story teller and a damn good journalist. Readers love your stories. Well?"

Carl, my Editor at the newspaper office in Victoria Street near Westminster Abbey, always ranted and ran his fingers through his thick white hair when he was under pressure. What pressure? I ask. Staff does all the work.

"I'll come up with something," I said. "Just can't get inspired. Need to think. Need somewhere to think."

"Right. I'll give you five days off. Go away somewhere. Think outside the box. Stay in a hotel. Just give me something. Five days and that includes the finished article. Three more than I should be giving you."

"Hope you are paying if I do decide on a hotel."

"Okay, okay. I'll sign off on the expenses," sighed Carl.

I left the office closing the door softly masking my annoyance.

Over lunch I pondered where I could go. My friend Delta couldn't contain her excitement. "Lucky you. Wish he had told me I could stay in a hotel for five days."

"Where do you think I should go? I've been going through the hotel lists and can't seem to find anywhere for inspiration."

Delta frowned then added brightly, "Go to one of the best and busiest. You know, people coming and going, that sort of thing."

After hugging my friend we departed. My head cleared and soon everything started falling into place.

I hesitated before booking into the "Elegancia" in the centre of Chelsea, knowing it was expensive, but then thought, what the heck, Carl was paying.

Today was Monday. I had until Friday to come up with something.

Arriving at the hotel, with just a carry bag, I had to set a plan in place if I was to get inspired so I asked the girl at the check-in desk if the hotel was busy.

"Oh yes," replied the receptionist. "We are almost full. You were lucky to get a room."

65

Good, I thought. I spotted her name tag and casually asked, "Any celebrities, government people, Russian spies perhaps, Andrea?"

Andrea laughed. "Can't tell you that. Wouldn't be worth my job. Confidentiality and all that."

A young Indian man approached me offering to carry my bag. I took my chances to quiz him.

Again reading his name tag I said, "So, Mani, how long have you been working here?"

"Six years. I love my job and it pays well. I am saving to marry my girlfriend some day," Mani answered. His face lit up as he talked, eager to tell me about his family back in India, babbling on until we reached the twentieth floor. I couldn't wait to write down what he said. Mani could prove to be a source of valuable information.

My room was small, decorated in white furnishings with shades of pale green and blue upholstery and cushions. What Delta would call "calming colours". The bath and white fluffy towels looked inviting, but there was work to do before I relaxed.

Taking out my laptop I booted up and jotted down interesting information so far. My plan was to have a paragraph on each person, situations, or whatever else cropped up and make this into a story. No time like the present.

Stepping into the lift I encountered a young couple leaning against the back wall. Nodding hello I noticed they had already pressed the ground floor button, so stood back.

"I thought you said this hotel was one of the best," said the young woman.

"Well, it was recommended. I think it is rather nice. The room is clean and comfy. What more do we need?" the young man replied.

"Clean and comfy! I want that and more. Much more for our honeymoon. Where's the opulence?" she said in a raised voice.

"Sorry, love, can't afford opulence."

Silence reined as she huffed herself into the corner.

My heart went out to this young man who seemed to be trying to meet his new wife's demands. Honeymoon hasn't got off to a great start.

Alighting from the lift I looked around for the least obvious seat in the lobby, somewhere I could watch what was happening around me. Spying a couch, tucked away beside a pillar, I walked over to make sure I had a good view of the lobby and reception desk. It was a perfect spot. Sitting down I discreetly put my notepad and pen on my lap, feeling I needed a sleuth cap and spyglass.

It was nearly five o'clock. Most guests had already checked in and were looking forward to their evening meal.

The self-opening entrance doors opened. A young man hurried in, pulling a little girl about five years old behind him. In his other hand was a brown slightly battered suitcase. Panting and looking distressed, he stopped at the desk as I strained to hear what he said. I managed to catch the words, double room, single beds, and two nights. The little girl kept yelling, "Where is Mum? I want Mum!"

"Shoosh. Mum's not here."

"I'm hungry. Where's Mum?"

"Come on. I'll show you our nice room and then we will get something yummy for dinner."

This seemed to quieten her as they disappeared into the lift. Something is going on there. I jotted down "Where is Mum?"

The second lift opened and an elderly couple arm in arm alighted and crossed the foyer, heading for the entrance.

Stopping suddenly, the lady exclaimed, "Oh no, I must have left my handbag in our room."

"No dear, you had it with you. Don't you remember I gave you the door card for safe keeping," replied her husband.

"Oh yes. I do remember. I put the bag down on the floor of the lift to adjust my scarf. There was that young man in the lift with us. He got out on the first floor. Oh no! Did he pick up my bag?"

They hurried back to the same lift pushing the button several times, willing the lift to open, before almost falling inside. I could see there was no bag on the floor.

Do I go to help them? Perhaps alert security staff? I waited what seemed an eternity before I decided to alert the girl on reception. Just as I did the lift door opened and the elderly couple came up to the desk visibly upset.

After telling the story to the receptionist, saying they would recognize the young man, she alerted the security officer who immediately went up to the first floor. He knew by the description of the man which room he was staying in.

In no time the officer was back holding the man firmly by the arm and clutching the lady's bag.

The police were called. In no time the man was whisked off in the police van and the lady had her handbag back.

By this time the hotel manager was on the scene and praised the staff for their prompt response.

Good time to ask for a raise. That's what I'd do.

After all this excitement I was starving, so headed back to my room to change for dinner. Not wanting to draw attention to myself I decided on simple black pants, my new cream shirt and my chunky emerald necklace. I stood back from the long mirror taking in my reflection. I was average height and weight with long blond hair, at the moment pulled back into a pony tail with a pretty clasp. My brown almond-shaped eyes were my best asset. The girls in the office envied my looks but I had my doubts and fears about myself. No different from anyone else really. Nearly twenty-two, I hadn't had a serious boyfriend as I forged ahead with my career. This assignment at the hotel could be the making of me.

At nearly six thirty I entered the dining room and saw the room was crowded but the waitress showed me to a vacant small table near a window looking out to the street. I settled in with a glass of red, as no one had said, "Don't drink on the job," and studied the menu.

A commotion from the kitchen disturbed my concentration. Voices were raised and the waitresses cast concerned glances between themselves. I couldn't hear what was actually being said, only hoped my dinner wasn't going to be cancelled by some chef getting upset.

After ordering a substantial meal of prawn entrée, followed by roast chicken and vegetables then finishing up with apple pie, I subtly asked the waitress was there a problem in the kitchen and would my order be filled.

"Oh yes, no problems. Just a small misunderstanding with the chef and staff," she replied with... was that a wink? Perhaps we could become friends, I chuckled to myself.

By now my head was spinning. No, it wasn't the wine, so much had happened within a few hours.

First Mani, then the honeymoon couple, followed by the father and crying little girl. The handbag incident came next and now the row in the kitchen. What had upset the chef?

Thinking of the crying little girl, there they were over in the corner eating dinner.

The child was passive now and enjoying herself. The father looked relieved and relaxed. How could I impose myself with a delicate question to him, where is the mum? Uhmm, bit presumptuous. There was a spare seat at their table. Refolding my napkin several times. I murmured, think girl, think.

My dinner turned out to be delicious bringing back memories of Mum's cooking. How long had she been gone now? Tears pricked my eyes as I tried to stop them trickling down my cheeks. The pain of losing her was still raw and emotions came quickly. Wiping my eyes with a tissue I thought I had better exit the dining room before I made a fool of myself. Smiling weakly at the waitress, I absentmindedly walked past the father and child. My foot suddenly caught in the leg of the spare chair causing me to stumble forward almost landing in his lap.

"Oh, my God, sorry, so sorry." The words tumbled out.

I had caught the father off guard and he automatically grabbed me from falling over, his hand brushing my left breast.

Struggling to my feet we both looked at each other in embarrassment whilst the little girl giggled at the incident.

"Please, sit down and recover," said the father.

Sinking down into the chair, I did in fact have to recover my composure. Am I really sitting here?

I managed a "thank you," as the young man poured me a glass of water.

Seeing my red eyes, he asked me if anything was wrong and could he help in any way. His look of concern made my heart jump. I couldn't help noticing a lock of dark hair falling on his forehead giving him a boyish look although he would have been around thirty. Concerned blue eyes looked at me questioningly, waiting for my reply.

"My mum passed away recently and the delicious roast dinner I had just now reminded me of her cooking. They are really tears of happiness as well as sadness."

The little girl looked at me with wide eyes and I could see a tremble on her lips as she whispered, "Everyone says my mum is in a place called Heaven. Is this where your mum went? Uncle Duncan told me again tonight, didn't you, Uncle?"

So, he is not her father. Why is she here with him?

Reading my thoughts he introduced himself saying, "Yes, I'm Duncan Foster. This is Cassandra, although everyone calls her Cassy."

Extending my hand I said, "I'm Carole Atkins. Sorry for your loss. Was she your sister, or..."

He cut me off saying, "No, my sister-in-law. My brother Peter's wife. He suddenly had to come here to Chelsea on a business trip and asked me to come too and look after Cassy as there's no one else. I've taken a few days off work to help out. We didn't travel together and I can't understand why he hasn't arrived at the hotel."

Saying goodnight I excused myself and left the dining room feeling quite embarrassed after the incident at the table. The lobby was empty and the receptionist was busy on the phone. Needing fresh air I walked outside. I chose to stand on the steps of the hotel within the flooding light. I could hear voices coming through the darkness and strained my eyes and saw the chef, just outside the tradesmen's entrance to the kitchen, in an animated conversation with someone wearing a full length coat and large hat pulled down. It was too dark to see whether it was male or female. The chef's voice rose angrily, "It's too much!" The coated figure turned and walked my way as the chef went inside. As the figure drew near I stepped back and just for a second the hat tilted and eyes met mine. I shivered even though the air was warm.

What was too much? Drugs perhaps?

Shaking my head I returned to my room. Finally I was able to run a bath instead of the quick showers. I was enjoying using the fluffy towels. Sinking into the warm water scented with the fragrance on offer, I closed my eyes and started to relax. My thoughts drifted to Duncan and Cassy. Perhaps there is a story there but is it wrong to intrude into their personal life? Still, I am a journalist.

The knocking on the door brought me out of my daze. Damn. Who's that? Just when I'm getting warm and comfortable. Wrapped in a towel I dripped my way to the door and peered through the security viewer. It was Duncan.

"I won't be a moment," I called as I ran back to the bathroom, dried myself off and scrambled into my jeans and t-shirt. Glancing in the mirror my hair looked a mess but I couldn't leave him standing outside for too long. I opened the door. "Sorry," I mumbled. "I was in the bath."

"I'm sorry to have disturbed you, but I'm hoping you can help me."

Not knowing whether to let Duncan in or not, I chose to talk to him at the door saying, "What's wrong? What's happened? Where's Cassy?"

Duncan held up to hand to silence my questions. "Cassy is asleep so I can't stay long. My brother has finally arrived and it seems he has his girlfriend with him." He looked up and down the passage as if he imagined she would materialize.

"Come in," I finally said. "Tell me what's going on. Why do you want my help?"

Sitting on the couch he poured out the story of how his brother was having an affair whilst his wife was critically ill. He wanted him to bring Cassy here in Chelsea where the girlfriend lives but not stay with them, so hence the hotel arrangement. All this under the pretext he was here on business. Furthermore his brother wanted him to stay just two more days while he sorted out his life.

"I run an architecture firm and I'm desperate to organize work for two prospective clients. If I don't submit a contract to them by Wednesday, which only gives me forty-eight hours, I'll lose their business."

"So how can I help you?" I asked.

"Could you, would you, look after Cassy tomorrow for the whole day. She is really taken with you. She chatted away about how pretty you were after you left the dining room."

"Oh dear, I don't know. I haven't had any experience looking after children. Also I'm on assignment for my newspaper. I've got to produce a story within the next four days."

Frowning he said, "I see. Never mind, sorry to have bothered you. I'll sort something out." Duncan looked despondent.

"I wonder if the hotel has a child minding facility. You could ask them." I was trying to smooth over my decline as best I could.

Duncan brightened up saying, "Yes, why didn't I think of that. I'll phone the reception now and find out."

He headed for the door, stopped and turned back saying, "Thanks anyway, perhaps you would like to join us for dinner tomorrow night. We can tell you what happened."

"That would be lovely. I'll see you in the dining room around six pm, if that suits you."

Later, propped up with pillows in bed, I added more information on my laptop. When am I going to start this story?

Next morning as I headed down for breakfast I encountered the honeymoon couple in the lift. This time the young woman smiled and clung to the man in obvious affection. I felt a pang of jealousy.

Guests had to go through the lobby to the dining room and I was startled to see four policemen in animated conversation with the manager. Mani was putting suitcases onto a trolley. I went over and asked him what was happening.

"My, my. What a shock. What a tragedy."

"What is, Mani?"

"Boris, our chef Boris. He been murdered. Waitress Mary found his body outside kitchen door this morning. He dead." Mani buried his head in his hands.

"Sit down somewhere for a while. I'm sure no one will mind," I said softly.

Well, this is interesting, very interesting. Steady on girl, think this through. Will I go over and tell the police what I saw last night? Or just let sleeping dogs lie? The coated figure may have had nothing to do with this, and beside, you can't give an accurate description.

The receptionist informed all guests the police wanted to interview everyone so no one was to leave the hotel.

Great. Now what do I do?

My turn to be interviewed came straight after breakfast. The policeman kept writing notes as I told him my story, adding that I wouldn't be able to identify the person.

"Long coat and large hat eh, sounds more like a female figure to me," he said studying my face.

"Could be," I answered. I had deliberately left out seeing the eyes of the person. For heaven's sake girl, get a grip. You've been watching too many crime movies!

Time to do some detective work myself.

Leaving the policeman to his next interview I asked at reception if they had a child minding area in the hotel.

"Oh, yes, we do," replied the young lady who had just come on the morning shift. "It is located on the fifth floor at the front of the building. Nice wide windows for the children to see out."

"Thanks."

Getting out of the lift I could see the sign on the door, so entered and approached the desk asking the lady if a little girl called Cassy Foster was there today.

"Are you her mother?"

"Oh no, I'm a friend of the family. Will her uncle would be back later on today to pick her up?"

On hearing this the lady could tell I was genuine. "Yes, Mr. Foster is coming around five o'clock. Can I have your name to tell him you were enquiring about Cassy?"

"I'm Carole Atkins; he'll know who I am."

Going back down to the lobby I saw the police were still asking questions. I noticed the waitress who was on roster in the restaurant the previous evening waiting to be interviewed. She looked nervous and kept tugging at her ponytail and straightening her jacket. She had heard the commotion in the kitchen and the chef yelling, what was that about?

I watched as the policeman spoke to her, only for a few minutes, then he dismissed her and she hurried past me. I caught up with her near the rear staff entrance.

"Excuse me, can I have a word?"

The waitress stopped. "Yes, how can I help?" she said politely, thinking I wanted "guest" information.

"I left my scarf on the chair where I was sitting having dinner last night and wondered if you handed it in somewhere, reception perhaps?" The words just rolled off the lie.

"No, didn't see it. Excuse me, I must hurry."

"Wait, you look distressed. Can I help? I heard the commotion in the kitchen last night and wondered if there was a connection with Boris's death."

"No, no! I can't say. It's all too much, the police, everything." She burst into tears.

Putting my arm around her I guided her through the rear door and onto a bench outside. For the first time I noticed her name badge which was partly hidden under her jacket.

"Calm down, Rose. I'm sure the police would have detained you if they suspected anything. Tell me what happened."

Rose looked cautiously at me as she composed herself. "I didn't tell the police everything as I don't want to get involved."

Then the whole story poured out. Boris was on drugs but was trying to get free of them. Drug dealers kept harassing and threatening him. They were very powerful people and made trouble for everyone. "So you understand I don't want any trouble."

I knew drug dealers were powerful, always eluding the police, alibis being created, and other dealers waiting in the wings to take over if anyone was caught.

"I do understand, Rose. I'm a journalist and come across news like this all the time."

"What?" She looked terrified. "Please, please don't quote me on what I just said. Leave me alone!" Almost leaping off the bench she ran away without a backward glance.

Don't worry, Rose; this may just be an "age old story" anyway. There's one nearly every day.

I arrived at the dining room around six o'clock to find Duncan and Cassy at a table by the window. I was glad I had taken the time to shower, carefully apply makeup and arrange my hair in an upward style. Looking in the long mirror wearing my blue silk shirt and white jeans I felt the effort was worthwhile.

"Hello, you're looking lovely tonight," said Duncan.

"I love your sparkly earrings," giggled Cassy. "Uncle Duncan thinks you're very nice."

Nice! I want more than very nice. I want wonderful, sexy, beautiful and fun to be with. Oh well.

"Did your meeting go well today?"

"Actually it did go very well," answered Duncan. "I was on Skype with the clients. They've decided to go ahead with their plans for the apartment building. Busy work schedule ahead."

"Is there a Mrs Foster included in this schedule?" I laughed, hoping the question wasn't too obvious.

"No, I'm as single as it gets." He too laughed as he added, "and no, I'm not gay."

I was relieved when the meal arrived right at that moment and the three of us tucked in. I was surprised how relaxed Cassy was.

"So, Cassy, how did you enjoy your day playing with the other children?"

"We all had so much fun. We are going home soon—Mum is not coming back to our house. I can't go to be with her just now, but Dad said I can go later on." Duncan gave me a glance that said, I'll tell you about it later, and we continued on with our meal.

"Where do you live?" I asked.

"In the Lakes District, Ambleside to be exact. Peter lives there too and Cassy goes to the local school. Wonderful area. Have you been there?"

"Yes, I went there for a holiday a couple of years ago. Loved the place."

"How is your writing coming along? Do you think you will have your story in a couple of days?" asked Duncan.

"Well, there certainly have been incidents since I arrived but I'm still hoping for something special."

"I noticed a small anteroom next door with children's toys. Let's take our coffee in there away from the noise, where we can talk," said Duncan.

I hadn't noticed this room but upon entering it felt welcoming with checked curtains and cushions. Books lined the shelves. The toys were in large box and in no time Cassy was playing on the floor building a Lego dolls house.

Duncan and I settled in on a sofa and he told me the recent developments.

"Peter is coming back here to collect Cassy tomorrow. Seems he has worked out things with his girlfriend, Matilda and for now he is taking Cassy back to Ambleside. Fortunately he has realised that his first priority is Cassy and her welfare. If Matilda is a decent person she'll know this is the right decision for now and in time they will work out a permanent solution."

I nodded thoughtfully.

"Thank you for being here and listening."

"It always helps to talk about problems," I said.

He reached over and grasped my hand. I didn't take it away as he leaned forward and kissed me, first on the cheek and then on my lips. My first thought was, I could marry this man. Another kiss followed, then a long embrace. Not knowing quite what to say I mumbled, "Are you going back tomorrow with Peter?"

"I can stay an extra day if you'd like."

"After that kiss, I really want to get to know you better. Please stay." It was not like me to be so forward.

Duncan looked pleased. "I'll check with reception and see if I can book an extra night."

We parted company and back in my room I shook my head to make sense of what had just happened. Steady on girl, you don't know anything about this man. Once again I updated information on my laptop.

So what did I have so far? Mani becoming a source of information about the hotel but that was about all. The honeymoon couple seemed to have sorted out their differences. The handbag snatcher has been arrested and presumably not coming back. They were all sort of dead ends. So I have to concentrate on Boris's murder. Being stabbed in the chest could be the work of a man or woman. It doesn't take much force to thrust a knife into someone's heart. So who would do it? Has to be someone that a: knew Boris and his drug activities, and b: someone with opportunity near the kitchen door. I thought again about the person in the long coat. After looking into my eyes, then perhaps watched me go back inside, the person could have turned and gone back to the kitchen door and when Boris came out again, stabbed him. Boris may have been on the verge of informing the police of drug lord activities.

Next morning I went down to breakfast early. The dining room was not yet

74

open and as no one was around I walked into the kitchen where I was greeted with aromas of grilled bacon, onions and toast.

A young man, presumably an apprentice chef, called out to me from behind his work bench. "Hello, you can't come in here. Breakfast is not served yet."

"Oh sorry, I thought the waitress may have been in here, I want early breakfast."

"Not yet. Just sit outside."

"Can I ask you, what happened with Boris? What I mean is, who would want to kill him?"

"I dunno. Boris had his troubles. Everyone knows about the drugs now. He shouldn't have gotten mixed up with it all. Dangerous people out there. Spies everywhere when drugs are involved."

"Rose seemed very upset about it all too. I wonder if she knows more than she is telling the police."

"Rose was in love with Boris. It was because of her he wanted to get clean to have a life together."

"I see. Who else working in the hotel knew about all this?"

"I guess just about everyone. There's a new girl only just started this week on reception. She wouldn't know anything. Not yet anyway. Look lady, why all the questions? Are you a reporter or something? You'll have to go. I've got breakfast to prepare."

He turned his back on me, so I left.

After breakfast I wandered into the lobby in time to see Duncan, Cassy and, I presume, his brother Peter on the steps of the hotel. I hurried to the doors to see a taxi pull up and had just enough time to call out a goodbye to Cassy. She ran over to me and hugged my legs before getting into the taxi. Peter looked surprised and confused but after shaking Duncan's hand he then was in the taxi and away they went.

"We couldn't find you for Cassy to say goodbye. You weren't in your room."

"I went down to early breakfast. At least we had a chance to say goodbye, she's a dear little girl."

Walking back inside, Duncan said he had managed to book another night but had some appointments to attend to, and would catch up later in the afternoon. That suited me as I had more detective work to do. So what are the police doing all this time? They had disappeared from the lobby so I could only guess they had enough information to take back to the police station and piece it all together.

Back to my story for Carl. So much had happened quickly I had to update my laptop at every chance. One more day left. I showered and changed into my new jeans and a floral shirt putting my hair in a ponytail. I slipped my mobile into my back pocket but it felt uncomfortable so I transferred it to the side pocket feeling it fall deeper.

Going down to the lobby I noticed a new receptionist. Must be the new lady the young fellow in the kitchen told me about. She had her back to me but as I approached she turned and looked into my face. Oh my God! Those eyes. They were the eyes of the person in the long black coat. Was she involved? Did she in fact double back and stab Boris? These questions flashed through my mind in seconds.

She knew I recognized her. I backed away. She came from behind the desk to confront me, her eyes brimming with anger.

"Why are you looking at me like that? Do you recognize me?" she asked, hissing through clenched teeth.

"No, I mean yes. You passed me outside the hotel."

Leaning towards me she said, "Boris should've kept up his drug habit. I made good money from him. He said, 'no more.' That's why he got it. Telling me he wanted a fresh start with Rose. What! That sniveling little waitress. I should have got her too! She is the cause of all this, not me! I got this job here so I could keep an eye on what was happening. Stay out of it!

Her eyes were wild as she ranted and her voice rose hysterically high, yelling about drug dealers, pimps and groveling users. I looked around hoping someone heard her but there was no one. Where was everyone? My throat constricted in fear and when I tried to call out, nothing came. I kept backing away from her into the dining room as she loomed in front of me. Suddenly she produced a knife from inside her jacket and started poking it at me. Looking at the blade, I froze. Finally I turned and ran into the kitchen. She was too quick. I felt the thrust of the knife as it went into my arm tearing through the sleeve of my shirt.

I screamed and stumbled. "Help me help me!" But no one was there.

I managed to kick out. She fell to her knees and the knife fell to the floor. I looked frantically around for an escape. The blood oozed down my arm, I held the wound tightly. I could see the freezer room and headed for that. Almost collapsing inside I grabbed the door to close it but she was too quick and the door clanged shut then bolted from the outside. With a hysterical laugh she called out, "You can now freeze to death. No one will find you in time. You shouldn't have meddled."

Looking around I could see she was right. I tried the door and felt for an emergency button, if someone accidently locked themselves in the freezer, but it was so dark I couldn't see anything. It was freezing and the wound in my arm was still oozing. I started yelling for help hoping it wasn't fruitless. The kitchen staff wouldn't arrive for the dinner shift until later in the afternoon. By then it maybe too late. Think girl, think. I sank to the floor as my head was spinning. Blood dripped. It was then a felt my mobile phone in the pocket. Thank God! Quickly I retrieved it but the words "no signal" jumped out at me. Damn! There must be a security phone in here. Sitting up and with the light on my phone I gradually managed to stand and slowly moved around. Sure enough on the back wall was a phone. Lifting the receiver and pressing the emergency button I heard nothing but a quiet drill tone. Come on. Come on!

Finally the security answered. I blurted out what had happened and where I was.

The rest of the day was a blur: The freezer door opening, lying on a stretcher, someone saying they had arrested the receptionist who had confessed to everything and Duncan racing to the hospital to see me.

Three years later I reflect back on the days at the hotel, hospital and convalescing at my father's home. Duncan came up from Ambleside every chance he had to visit me. Our relationship blossomed and I fell hopelessly in love with him. The five days for the story to be finished flew out the window. Carl was happy to wait. I did eventually finish the story, embellishing a few points here and there, but hey, I'm a journalist aren't I? Delta was happy to edit it for me before it went to press.

Duncan's marriage proposal came out of the blue and even though we had only known each other a short while, we had been through so much together. I knew we would be happy. We married and now live in Ambleside. Duncan's architectural business is thriving and I'm working at the local newspaper. Cassy has become a big part of our lives. Matilda decided Peter wasn't for her and now after three years he is seeing a beautiful lady, Alison, who absolutely adores eight-year-old Cassy.

I love my life in Ambleside and have to pinch myself sometimes that it is all real! I still see Carl and Delta and we often laugh that if I hadn't needed to get away to find a story I would never have met Duncan.

Joyce Iles

The Unspoken

I stood with my sister on the roadside, where the car from the station had just left us. We stared at the house that stood before us.

The homestead nestled on the edge of the forest, a large rambling place that was sorely in need of repair. The iron roof was rusting, some of the windows were a little out of skew and the outhouses looked tumbledown. On the back wall stood two rainwater tanks, also a little rusted. Despite this, from a distance at least, it was an attractive sight fringed by the trees that were turning autumn colours.

Jane, two years younger than me, looked a little scared. "It's old and creepy looking," was her comment.

There was no one outside to welcome us, so we stood for a while, taking it in. We were used to life in the city, so hoped we would find things to occupy our time for the next four weeks.

Our parents had gone away for a holiday in England and had arranged for us to stay here during this time. This was the home of an aunt and uncle who we had met only a handful of times, so they were virtually strangers to us. Even I, who was just in my teens, felt a little apprehensive about spending such a long time with family members we hardly knew.

As we stood gazing at the tumbledown house, an old dog came shambling towards us, a household pet obviously, as well as perhaps a guard dog. The animal regarded us and appeared neither friendly nor surly. Those old teeth wouldn't do a lot to deter anyone, I thought.

Shortly afterwards, our aunt appeared with our uncle trailing in her wake. "Hello, you're here then," my aunt said a little gruffly. "Don't worry about the dog, he won't bite you," she added.

"Hello, girls. Glad to see you got here safely. Some of those drivers at the station tend to be a bit gung-ho on these country roads." This comment came from our uncle who had caught up with our aunt by this time. He at least sounded a tad friendlier.

They gathered up our meagre belongings and walked with us to the front of the house. We entered and looked around tentatively. The inside looked about as old as the outside, but it was clean and had a sort of well-worn charm about it.

They showed us around the house and explained that we would be sharing a room. We didn't mind a bit, in fact we were quite glad we would have each other's company during the night, especially in a strange and rather old house.

We were left to our own devices while we unpacked our clothes and settled into our new surroundings. Along with some clothes there were a few items for our amusement—our favourite books and games as we supposed our aunt and uncle would not have any such items suitable to occupy our time.

I wondered why they didn't have any children of their own and voiced this question to Jane. "Just as well," she answered, "they would probably be rather grumpy parents."

"Don't be unkind. It was nice of them to have us while Mum and Dad are away."

"I suppose so. I don't know why Mum and Dad couldn't have taken us with them."

"I think they had some business to settle, so it isn't really going to be a much of a holiday for them, and we'd most likely be in the way. We'll just have to make the best of things while we are here."

We ate lunch with Aunt Esther, our mother's older sister, although they seemed nothing alike. Our uncle had gone into town on an errand and wouldn't be back until much later. We ate mostly in silence, although our Aunt tried to make conversation by asking about our school and other activities. We did our best to liven up the atmosphere and hoped things would improve as we got to know them.

When Uncle Dan arrived home he spent some time in a discussion with Aunt Esther and later they joined us.

"We thought you might like a trip into town in a day or so, once you've settled in here," our uncle said. "Not that there is a lot to see. You might meet one or two kids of your own age. As it's vacation time now, you won't meet any at school."

"Sounds good. We might make one or two friends."

My aunt gave me a look. "We don't want the pair of you gadding about and making a nuisance of yourselves. I want you to spend most of your time here. I'm sure I can find things for you to do."

"Yes, Aunt Esther." We were beginning to feel trapped already.

The following day Uncle Dan showed us around their property. It was not huge but they had a fairly large area where they kept quite a few free-range chickens. Apart from using the eggs themselves, our uncle said he went into town once a fortnight and sold them to the store and a few of the townspeople.

They also kept a number of fruit trees and a large vegetable garden which added to their income. When the fruit and vegetables were in season, he kept a stand by the side of the road and sold the produce to passers-by.

Jane and I got to know how things worked around the house and property and although our life was none too exciting to date, we did our best to get along with our aunt and uncle. Aunt Esther was far less open with us than Uncle Dan. She didn't seem to like young people very much.

We finally had our trip into town and it proved to be just as my uncle had said. There was a pub, a general store, a shop that sold local arts and crafts, a clothing store and a café. There were a few other buildings but these were devoted to the sale of farm machinery and other items that my sister and I deemed "uninteresting".

We managed to speak to some kids who were roughly our age, while our aunt and uncle were making purchases in the general store.

"I'm Marion and this is my sister Jane," I volunteered to the kids who stopped to say hello to us. "We're staying with our aunt and uncle while our parents are away."

Our newly-found friends looked at each other immediately with a darting glance.

"Oh! We hope you like it out there. We don't know your aunt very well. She doesn't come into town very often. Both seem a bit strange, but that's probably because we haven't had a lot to do with them," they hastened to say, not wanting to appear rude.

"We don't know them at all well either," I said. "We've only met them a few times. Here they are now, so we had better go. Hope we see you around again soon."

We spent some time looking in the art and craft shop and hoped our aunt would suggest going into the café for a milkshake or ice-cream, but it didn't work out that way. I suppose not having children of their own, they didn't have much idea of what kids liked to do.

After spending a few hours in town we returned home and spent the rest of the day reading and playing games. We offered to take the dog, Rupert, for a walk and Aunt Esther begrudgingly agreed to this.

"He's rather old, so don't try and hurry him along. He likes to go at his own pace. Don't go too far and get lost in the bush."

"Fine," I said. "We'll stick to walking along the road."

We took a ball along with us so we could have a game with Rupert, who by now had rather taken to us. We tossed the ball to him as we walked and chatted together as we went, waiting for the dog to bring it back and then repeating the process. This activity continued for a while until Rupert failed to return with the ball. We called out to him a number of times and eventually heard him barking.

Running towards the sound, we found him scratching around in the soil, a considerable way from the road, although it was still within the boundary of our uncle's property.

"What have you found, Rupert?" asked Jane, as we ran towards the dog.

His only reply was another woof!

After reaching the spot where Rupert stood, we peered at the ground and gasped when we saw what held the dog's interest. Lying in a shallow recess, I could see immediately what appeared to be a pile of bones. One of these most certainly looked like a human skull, though very small.

"We'd better go and tell Aunt Esther," I said to Jane. She nodded with a look of alarm.

Jane and I attached Rupert's leash to his collar and led him back to the house. Our aunt appeared at the door when we arrived.

"That walk didn't last long. What happened?"

"Rupert loved us throwing the ball to him, but he came across some bones buried in the ground. We thought they may be human bones, but they're very small," I said in a rush.

Aunt Esther suddenly turned white and let out a shriek. "What have you done?" she screamed at us, and continued screaming until Uncle Dan came running to the door.

"What's going on?"

"They found her. They dug up her bones. My little baby girl."

She collapsed sobbing and was led away by our uncle. We were left stunned, not knowing what to do, so sat on the front doorstep close to each other without speaking for some time, unable to think of anything to do that might help.

At last Uncle Dan appeared and asked us to come into the house. We got up slowly and followed him. He beckoned us to sit and he sat in a chair before us.

"I'm sorry this has happened," he said. "It's not your fault so don't feel bad; it was bound to happen sooner or later I guess."

He sighed and continued speaking, "Not long after we moved here your aunt fell pregnant. We were both so happy, as we had longed for a child and thought we were never going to be blessed in this way. This turned out to be correct I'm afraid. The baby started coming one night when it was close to her term. The town is some distance away and there is no doctor available. We had to deal with the matter ourselves. Unfortunately, our little girl was stillborn. It broke our hearts and your aunt has never really got over this trauma. We buried the baby ourselves near a special tree, but obviously over the years the ground in which she lies has become washed away with the rain. The grave wasn't marked as we had not told anyone we were expecting a child, so we have kept this a secret all these years."

On hearing this very sad account of this episode in their lives we wept.

"We're just so, so sorry," was all we could manage to say.

"Well," said Uncle Dan, "perhaps it's just as well it's out in the open. Your aunt and I might be able to get over the guilt of keeping this a secret all this time."

He left the room and went back to comfort Aunt Esther.

Much later when we were getting ready for bed Aunt Esther came into our room. She seemed a little different now and looked at us searchingly before speaking.

"I'm sorry for my outburst a while back. I should have let go of this a long time ago, but I felt so guilty for not being able to give my husband the family he wanted. I kept it all a secret from everyone, including your mother and spent a good part of my life shutting out people because I was ashamed of my actions. I would've healed better if I had shared my grief with the family."

"We're sorry that you've been unhappy and we promise we will never let anyone know what happened here," I assured our aunt. "It will be our secret too."

Jane and I both stepped forward a little hesitantly and put our arms around her. Our aunt responded to our warmth and hugged us in return, shedding some tears again.

As time wore on, the tense atmosphere in the house gradually faded away and we all began to enjoy each others company, even having a few laughs from time to time. I think my aunt was now regretting the years she had wasted, grieving over something she could never change and was now prepared to move on and live again.

It came time for us to leave their home as our parents had returned from England. Mum and Dad drove up to her sister's home and we all spent some time together before returning to the city.

As we finally said our farewells, Jane and I actually felt sad to say goodbye to Aunt Esther and Uncle Dan.

Our aunt's departing words to us were, "Please come and stay with us again sometime soon."

We assured them both that we would indeed.

Sue Palmer

The Storybook Quilt

Jan placed the basketful of clothes she had just removed from the line on a bench in the family room. She sighed to herself, clothes to sort and fold, ironing waiting to be the done, dinner to prepare, always something requiring attention. Feeling a little weary she sat down on a sofa. A colourful patchwork quilt was draped over the back of it.

Reaching out, Jan gently traced her fingers over a few of the squares. Her mother Kate had sewn the quilt many years ago, her choice of fabrics, colours, stitching and embroidery work told a story. Each square captured a special memory from her life and some squares that her children would recall from their childhood, she called it her "Storybook Quilt".

The thistle-and-tartan block always held a special memory for Jan as her mother's birthplace had been Scotland and she loved this link with her heritage. On another she saw tartan music notes and knew they symbolised bagpipe music and music played by the Scottish Highland Fiddle Orchestra. Jan examined the detailed stitching on a patch that pictured tall, towering trees; she knew it represented forest in the deep South West of Western Australia.

Her parents had been part of the Early Group Settlement scheme, given a parcel of land in Witchcliffe to clear and farm. The number fifty-two was stitched on a square and it held a wealth of meaning to those early pioneers who formed part of that particular group. Life was tough, crude and frequently cruel. There was no escape from the scorching heat of summer, fear of bushfires and the flies, always the flies. The cold winds in winter blew relentlessly and chilled to the bone, to walk anywhere meant trudging through thick, sticky mud that clung to shoes, boots—anything. Jan was thankful to live in modern times along with the technology now taken for granted.

Kate's husband tragically passed away and in time she re-married, moving with her husband and children to a farming community north of Perth in the Wheatbelt. One of the patchwork squares pictured a rustic, barbed wire fence with woolly

83

sheep in the background, and another a field of wheat. Jan fondly remembered the vast, wide open spaces of the farm, swimming in the farm dam with mud underfoot. Running down tracks where rain had cut channels of flowing puddles of water along the fence- line, not for them the tiny backyards children are confined to today. She recalled milking cows, just a stool, bucket and a strong, clean pair of hands were all that was needed. The odd cow had a quirky temperament you had to be aware of, such as a well-aimed kick in your direction.

A patchwork square was covered in small pink and yellow flowers. Jan along with her sisters had picked handfuls of these rustling paper daisies to tie up and dry upside down in the kitchen. Later they would be a splash of colour in an empty jam tin sitting on the window sill. She looked closely at a square of a rough farm cottage with wispy smoke curling sky woods from the chimney. She recalled the warmth of the farm kitchen, having to carry in wood for the fire and the smells and delights that came out of the oven. Microwave cooking today doesn't quite evoke the same warmth in creating and sharing memories.

On the quilt was a cleverly embroidered square of a wooden wheel from a cart. Jan smiled as she recalled the means by which she and her siblings had travelled to the little country school. Horse and cart provided much more of an experience than air conditioned school buses of today. To this day, Jan still felt an affinity with horses, particularly Clydesdales.

A square, resembling stained glass with a cross worked into the patterned fabric reminded Jan of the tiny country church the family attended. Other patches held the names of each of Kate's children. She thought about her children and the unique nature and character of each child. They were growing up too quickly.

Sometimes the hustle and bustle of life gets in the way, the tyranny of the urgent takes the place of more important things. She would endeavour to build in more time to share memories captured in her precious quilt with her family.

There were a number of blank squares in the quilt; Jan looked forward to working with her daughters to create stories of their own. Making and recording these memories in some meaningful way is so important for future generations. It anchors them to the past providing a sense of time, place and belonging, a pictorial heritage to be passed on to the next generation. "Thank you, Mum, for our Storybook Quilt," she softly whispered.

Carolyn Nelson

Old Salt

Five o'clock, the storm-front heavy,
Dark and wet ... the wind gusts: cold,
Collar up ... his hat brim tilted,
Wearing shoes he'd had re-soled.
Albert's call-out was a hard one,
His arthritic hands were sore
From hauling on the salt-wet ropes
On a dock, not quite secure.
His sea-legs served him well today,
As the wooden dock had swayed,
The harsh sea fighting with the ship,
Had the younger men afraid.
But not Albert ... an old sea-dog,
Body swaying with the dock,
He hauled in ropes thrown by deck-hands,
His feet planted like a rock.
Mooring ships in such harsh weather,
Albert took it in his stride,
And no matter what it cost him ...
It was done! With skill and pride.
Though his battered hands were bleeding,
And his back; in screaming pain,
When they called him out for rescue ...
He would answer, once again.

Lynne Tatam

Escaped Animals

Some idiot left open the zoo's main door
Animals stampeded across the floor
The chimps screamed and bounced around
Flinging their poo at the inner compound

Lions chased the panicking giraffe
Heads would roll for this massive gaffe
People sacked, jobs will go
If we kept quiet no one need know

Meerkats fled into the tigers' lair
They were flung and tossed high in the air
Squeaking they flew into outer space
Winding up limply in the tiger's face

One by one they were each rounded up
By the promise of food from an eating cup
We were pretty sure we'd caught them all
Until we glanced at the brown bears' stall

The bruins it seemed had completely fled
Were they alive? Or worse yet dead!
The sound of snoring assailed my ears
Sleeping soundly lay all seven bears

No one knew what happened that day
When all the animals escaped to play
We kept very quiet and managed to smile
But where was that bloody crocodile?!

Terry Duhig

Chaotic and Rocky

Leaving the garage, I opened the laundry door and made my way into the kitchen. Laura's head turned to face me, a large knife was held upwards as she came towards me, her free hand brushed the front of her apron, small fragments of a variety of vegetables fluttered to the floor. She was smiling, and as they always have done, her smiles caused her cheeks to rise and fill out giving her, what I think, is a mischievous look; we came close and with both her arms stretched out wide, she pouted her lips to be ready and waiting for that big greeting kiss.

With my arms encircling her waist, our lips met, they stayed pressed together for our usual five second passion event, this was followed by her regular question to me, which is, "And how's my gorgeous lover boy, had a good day?"

"Don't ask," I replied.

She stepped back with a frown on her face, her eyebrows rose and she knew what to say. "George beat you again, didn't he?"

"Yup, stuffed it up on the eighteenth, even stevens till then; my nerves got the better of me, my approach went into the lake, his landed two foot short of the hole. Cost me a tenner." I put on a sad, self-pitying, long faced expression telling her that.

She had her shoulders give a shrug, turned and went back to her cutting board. "Storm warning on the telly, due this evening; roast beef, Yorkshire pudding and the works for dinner, I'll give you a shout when I need a meat slicer."

Good, Sunday dinner cooked to perfection, the thought of that replaced my dismal announcement of a few seconds earlier in my mind, and as I left the kitchen I told her that I would have a shower and get changed.

I still get chuffed and sort of amazed that she can always manage to say something that cheers me up and blows the blues away. Laura, the one who still loves me and makes me feel great every day.

It was the long roll of thunder that I heard as I was dressing, then the strong gust of wind that rattled our bedroom window, but the loudest noise was Brutus barking his darn fool head off; no lover of storms is Brutus, he may be the big Bull

Mastiff who scares the pants off strangers when he greets them at the front door, but thunder has him rattled every time, and he lets us know it, barking, barking, barking. The storm had arrived.

Entering the sitting room, lightning flashed, and even though the curtains were drawn it turned heads towards them; Jessie was at the computer, she stopped talking into her mobile.

Ralph looked up from the long card table, he was back at his Star Wars jigsaw once more, trying to finish it, didn't seem too many pieces left to put into place, he'd been at it, on and off, for the past two weeks. Brutus was racing around the sofa, no longer bursting his lungs advising one and all that a storm was overhead.

The kitchen door opened and my beloved appeared long enough to tell me that the joint needed carving, and to order the two younger members of our tribe to get their hands washed and get into the dining area, that dinner was ready. I walked towards her.

That was the moment; it was if Zeus was waiting up above the clouds for Laura to speak, for no sooner had her words departed from her lips, that was when he gave the order, a huge clap of thunder sounded right overhead. I thought I felt the house shudder, and then the lights went out; both the television and the computer screens shrunk to a dot and went blank. Jessie screamed; Ralph cursed loudly with a word that I do not want to hear from him again; the card table careered past me, jigsaw pieces flying in the air; Brutus was on the move, racing about the room, reacting to the storm; he continually barked.

I was next in line, standing just inside the dining area, doing my best to assess as to what on earth was happening, when, hearing the sound of a howl, I was instantly struck a tremendous blow and was hurtled forward; propelled by a leaping upward, lump of canine that had left the ground, his front outstretched paws clouted me in the middle of my back.

My unexpected travelling ceased when, with my legs and arms flailing, I crashed into the underside of the dining table, my head somehow passed safely between its legs, but my shoulders caught the table leaf and the table rose and staggered.

Lying face down on the kitchen tiles, my ears received a once in a lifetime noise mixture.

An obnoxious blend of a mother's scream together with a loud, very loud panic type continuous barking; a horrendous clap of thunder, directly overhead; both of our children yelling, screaming words that I could not comprehend; the ultimate, the unbearable worst noise of all, that of glass and crockery smashing, cutlery clattering and some other odd items striking a hard surface. All of these were entwined into an indescribable sound that was sustained for two to three seconds.

Then came my nightmare; lightning flashed and lit up everything around me, a scene that my eyes could not believe, one that will remain with me for years I fear; this was accompanied by a rush of pain, which had me groaning, my shoulders and back felt as though they were shattered.

This was much worse than losing at the eighteenth to George!

My Laura, she was calling my name, no, not calling, shouting my name, asking where was I and was I all right? I could hear her clearly because Brutus had suppressed his vocal chords and was making gulping noises instead, and, by some strange miracle, in spite of perceiving those sounds, I made out a conversation between my darling children, even though it was occurring at a screaming pitch.

Jessie screamed at Ralph, "You stupid, idiotic big-footed imbecile, you trod on my fingers, you crushed them into the carpet, get away from me, well away!"

"What in hell's name are you crawling around on the floor for? And don't call me an idiot, it's idiots that go around crawling on all fours in the dark," Ralph was advising her with his volume control turned up as far it would go.

"I'm trying to find my mobile, I dropped the rotten thing when that thunder made me jump, listen don't move, stand still, you might tread on it and smash it." This was a change in tone, she sounded almost tearful.

"Hang on, I'll creep over to the window and open the curtains, lightning flashes could let you see it," his voice lowered, calm and compassionate.

"No!" Jessie shouted, "Don't move, don't move." Definitely panicking now.

"Too late, I've gone," his calm response.

"I'm under the table, Laura my love, give me a moment, get the torch from the cupboard above the sink; and have you any idea what on earth is Brutus eating?"

I started to wriggle backwards, still lying flat, trying my damnedest not to aggravate the pain level still emanating from my upper body.

"Stay there, darling; I think broken glass and crockery is all around you, stay still till I get the torch. I can hear Brutus and fear the worst; we may have to buy fish and chips."

Her words gave me comfort, well not exactly comfort, but I felt a little better hearing her talk. I stopped wriggling because a loud bang followed by a crashing noise filled my ears, those sounds came from the living room; next came a spate of swear words from Ralph, which I shall refuse to describe. When the swearing ceased, I shouted at the living room, it was almost echoed, I think it was Jessie also shouting similar words to what I did.

"What in Heaven's name is going on in there?"

"The curtain rod broke, Dad, it fell on me, the curtains are on the floor, all I did was pull on them; hey, outside, it's dark all over the place, no street lights or anything; across the road seem to have torches flashing about in their house.

There's still lightning, but its further away now; can we have our torch in here?" Ralph updated us all with his news.

"The torch, someone moved the torch, it's not where it usually is," as my wife, she informed me in a calm manner. Then she changed to a mother demanding an answer by shouting past me, "One of you moved the torch, where did you put it, I need it now, answer me, where the hell did you put it?" Desperation had now assumed control.

Replies came immediately, one after the other, both denying touching the torch and not offering any suggestions as to its whereabouts. Mother grunted several times, "Huh!"

The mystery attached to the torch lasted within the next minute.

"Got it, someone put a book in here and knocked the darn thing over; it was behind a book!" Her statement was shouted with glee.

She switched it on, for a beam of light shot across the kitchen.

Magic happened! Amazingly the house lights came back on at the same moment. That had me considering whether I should go out and buy a couple more of those fantastic torches.

Not prepared to take chances, I swept my arms around slowly, my fingers gliding across the kitchen tiles, satisfied that no broken glass or crockery would be encountered, I sat up; wrong move! For I also gained attention from Brutus, he obviously was overjoyed at seeing me, for the next thing I knew he was licking my face.

Roast beef flavoured licks; bits, remnants of a roast joint fell in my eyes and in my mouth.

Another loud noise came from the sitting room; it wasn't what I needed, not at that moment. The television sound was blaring and it sounded awful, screaming voices with a backing of twanging instruments; for sure, it wasn't my kind of music.

It was too much, after what we all had just been through, so I yelled out, "Turn that rubbish off, NOW!"

Ralph appeared in the doorway, he was goggle-eyed at what he saw on display everywhere, but it was only a brief distraction, for he quickly turned to face a slobbering Brutus and presumably realised that his dear old Dad was in a prone position behind him, because he desperately said, "Let me leave it on, Dad, I've waited all week for this, it's the Rocky Horror Show!"

Pamela Poole

The Sea Wind

The sea wind stirs the chimes above my head. I do not see the wind but I hear its voice. The soft sea wind that moves the grasses in long flowing waves passing along the dunes, just as the sea waves move on the face of the ocean.

If I were to sink into the grass would it be like sinking into the sea? Such strange thought must be brought by the sea wind that stirs the chimes above my head, as I sit in my chair at the end of the day. The soft sea wind with its salty breath, what memories it must gather in its journey over the limitless oceans. Let me hear those secrets as the chimes stir above my head.

Let me dream of whales and dolphins, fish of rainbow beauty, and caves of darkest blue. I feel the soft sea wind on my face as I rest in my chair at the end of the day and the chimes stir gently with the passing sound of the secrets of the sea.

Balancing Act

I took a deep breath, steeling my courage to take another step. My arms gripped the pole firmly, holding it perfectly horizontal in front of me, and I took another step, careful not to look down. I knew what was awaiting me below, but I had been walking tightrope as long as I could remember; I would be fine.

"Hey, Sweatervest, I need your help with something." The voice startled me from my thoughts and I looked up.

"Yes, Helen?" I asked, a polite smile on my face. Helen and Elle were my best friends, I hung with them every day.

"I need some help with my homework," Helen explained. "Y'see, me and Dad were going to the car show, and I'll run out of time to do it. You don't mind, do you?" My pole tilted slightly to one side, and I shifted my weight; Helen never did her homework if she could help it, nothing I couldn't handle. "Thanks." She smiled, leaving me with her stuff.

"Me too, Lissie!" Elle called out. "Help me out too." Again I felt my weight shift, and with careful calculations, I righted myself; I could handle this easily. I kept my sights ahead of me, everything carefully poised, carefully planted.

"Yeah, sure ... I guess." My polite smile never wavered. Taking it one step at a time, I moved forward. I couldn't fall under, not yet.

"Thanks Lissie! You're the best!" Elle and Helen turned away from me when the teacher came in.

"Good afternoon class." He smiled widely at us. "Your results from last week's paper came in. Most of you—as usual—passed." He started walking between the rows of desks, handing students their papers. He put mine on my desk, and looked disappointed. "You can do better, Lissie, I know you can." He shook his head. I swayed, feeling unsteady for a moment, but righted myself. This was always the case. Nothing unusual. I won't fall down. The teacher finished handing out the papers and stood at the front of the classroom, continuing on with his lesson, giving us yet another assessment piece.

Class ended and we were dismissed. I had to walk home, my parents weren't there to pick me up as usual. It took me half an hour and before I even stepped inside, I was already bombarded with questions such as "Why are you late?" and "What happened at school?" Just shrugging off the questions, I headed to my room but got stopped at the stairs.

"Oh, your cousin is coming over, but you'll need to babysit her for the night, because your father and I have to go out. Oh and make sure you get your homework done," my mother told me. I groaned and was instantly snapped at. "Don't take that tone with me, young lady! You graduate at the end of the year, and if you want to get into university, you better pass. You know, your second cousin who is younger than you is already planning her first year studies at university? And what do you aspire to be? You can't live with us for the rest of your life."

I could feel the other end of the pole getting heavier, but I took a breath and regained my balance. I could do this. I stayed silent, letting my mother speak. Finally she had finished, and I turned to leave.

"Don't forget to feed your cousin," my mother reminded me. "You should start cooking soon, she'll be here any moment and you know how picky she can be."

"Yes, Mother." I nodded with a smile, turning to the kitchen. Both sides of the pole were heavy, but it was nothing I couldn't handle. I took a breath and continued on.

I was nearly finished cooking when my cousin arrived. She came in and started chattering about her day. "And then he looked at me and smiled! He smiled! At me! Is there anyone that likes you? Oh wait ... nobody likes you, how could I forget?" She screeched. It was laughter. High-pitched laughter. The end began to tilt again, I had to shake away the negativity and press on.

We sat down and ate dinner, she picked at it, eating certain parts and ignoring the rest. My parents came down and kissed us goodnight, then left.

"Remember your homework, Lissie!" my mother called before the door closed. The other end tilted. It was heavy, and I was panting hard, but I continued to push on. Dinner was finally over and I did the dishes, before trying to get my cousin to settle. She just wouldn't. She kept wanting to play and wouldn't leave me alone. One am came and went and though I still hadn't gotten her to sleep, she was at least watching a movie, lying on top of me, and refusing to get off. I still had my homework, and my best friend's homework...

"Wake up, Lissie, you'll be late!" A strong wind caused me to teeter as I woke suddenly. I'd slept through the night... Oh no, I'd slept through the night! Jumping to my feet, I threw my clothes on and ran out the door. If I could get to school quickly, I could quickly do the homework. The wind blew stronger and I swayed on the tightrope again; I just had to make it.

The rest of the day felt like a blur. First I was late, then I was marked down for not having my homework. Helen got mad at me for not doing her homework, and Elle gave me those puppy dog eyes. Stepping through the door I was met by an unimpressed mother; apparently the school had called. By the time I got to my room, my head was spinning.

Tears welled in my eyes as the wind buffeted me around. I could do this! I had to do this!

My foot slipped.

Tears fell as I collapsed into bed. I was hanging to my tightrope by one hand, my pole in the other. The phone rang. I couldn't do this, not now.

"Elizabeth, you have a visitor!" came my father's voice. The pole began to slip.

"Lissie?" I didn't have to look up to know it was Elle. "Are you okay?" As I fell, I felt a strong hand grab hold of me. A pair of warm arms enveloped around me holding me tight. "I was worried," Elle explained. "I didn't want you to be sad."

"Let go." I could almost hear her say.

"I can't." I didn't reply.

"Lissie, please stop crying. I've got you." Elle simply held me. I had a choice to make. "I'm here if you need me. You can tell me what's wrong." Letting go of the pole, I let her pull me up.

"I can't do this alone anymore," I whispered.

"You're not alone," Elle whispered back. I looked up. She was holding me steady, helping keep my balance on the long tightrope of life. It wasn't easy, but I didn't have to be alone.

Anita Magee

Moments

Moments are not intended to remain,
It gives us the opportunity to do things again.
Ideal circumstances don't appear on silver platters,
It's how we decide individually what truly matters,
We all know love, success, loss and pain,
How we experience it is not the same,
What I know of you and you know of me,
Is already just but a memory.
In each moment lies the process of change,
In the past, present or future no one can remain.

Valerie Lee

The Princess and the Silkworm

In the ancient kingdom of Hotan there once lived a very cunning prince. His land nestled in the shadow of the mighty kingdom of China. Every week caravans from many distant lands passed through Hotan on their way to buy silk from China.

Now China and Hotan, at that time, lived in peace. One day, the Prince called for a messenger. "I will send you on a journey east," the Prince said to the messenger as he bowed to the floor. "You will carry a message to my noble friend, the Emperor of China. Tell the Emperor we humbly seek silkworm eggs and mulberry tree seeds to bring back to the Kingdom of Hotan."

"I fear the Emperor's reply," the messenger said as he bowed again. "I may lose my head. The Chinese emperors have kept the art of silk-making a deadly secret since time began. Silkworms are forbidden to leave China."

The Prince thoughtfully stroked his beard. "The Emperor of China smiles upon the Kingdom of Hotan. For many seasons, we have exchanged gifts in friendship. Make haste! I eagerly await his reply."

Soon after the full moon had risen four times, the messenger returned and showed himself again before the impatient Prince.

"His Imperial Majesty," the messenger spoke, "forbids all silkworm eggs and mulberry tree seeds to cross the borders of China. All travellers will be searched, and terrible punishment will be meted out those who disobey."

"I will find a way," the Prince replied. "For years tired travellers have passed Hotan seeking to buy the magical cloth of silk. I too wish to sleep in silken robes and make my people grow rich from selling silk."

The messenger ran from the angry Prince's sight. And the Prince sat upon his throne and thought. He frowned and frowned until his forehead became like a rice field of hills and furrows.

Finally, he once again called for his weary messenger. "We have heard the Emperor has a daughter of great beauty and wisdom. Tell the Emperor, I seek for my son, his daughter's hand in marriage. She will make a perfect bride."

Again, the messenger rode away to China and after the full moon had risen for the fourth time, he bowed once more before the Prince of Hotan. "Good news," spoke the messenger, "his Imperial Majesty agrees to the marriage. He is honoured our royal households will be joined together."

"Ah haa," nodded the Prince wisely. "We will send a splendid army to fetch her. Get my captain! I must speak with him alone before he leaves."

When the captain appeared before him, the Prince said, "You will have a very important mission. You must bring the Princess of China to Hotan safely. But, there is one thing you must do before she starts her journey to Hotan. You must seek her alone and give her a secret message from me."

The captain gave a very low bow, and said, "I am listening and will keep it close."

"Tell the Princess, the Prince of Hotan regrets she will rule in little else than wool and goat hair clothing. Here in Hotan we know not the way of silk-making because we have neither silkworms nor mulberry trees to feed the worms. Unless the Princess can bring with her the means of making silk she will never wear silk again."

Once again, the captain rode to China, while the Prince of Hotan waited in his palace for his people to return from yet another journey. And, just before the spring moon, a tired rider appeared before the Prince, announcing, "The Princess comes, but two days away."

"Sound the palace gong," the Prince shouted. "Make ready for the Imperial Princess. We will give her a grand welcome. We will play the trumpets and put flowers everywhere."

The Princess arrived, dressed in gold and red silken robes which shimmered like the setting sun. Her tiny face, like a pale rose, peeked from under a magnificent hat.

"I trust you had a safe journey," enquired the Prince as the Princess bowed before him.

"You give me great honour," the Princess replied. "I give you a gift."

Then to everyone's surprise she took off her hat. Her black hair fell like a dark shadow across her back. Two tiny packets made of silk spilled from inside her hat onto the ground.

"I bring you silkworm eggs and mulberry tree seeds," the Princess said. "I heard you had no silk in Hotan. It is unfitting that a royal Princess of China wear wool and goat hair. I will plant the mulberry tree seeds in the palace garden. When the silkworm eggs hatch, together the trees and silkworms will grow. When they spin a cocoon, I will show your people how we gather and weave silken thread."

"This is indeed a great day for Hotan," the Prince said. "All the people of Hotan will remember your bravery in bringing us the way of silk-making."

"It is true," the Princess replied. "Even I would have lost my head if they knew I carried the silkworm eggs and mulberry tree seeds out of China. But, at the border the guards feared to search a royal princess. How wise that you asked me to bring the seeds," said the princess as she gave the prince a secret smile.

The Princess kept her promise to the kingdom of Hotan. She planted the mulberry tree seeds in the palace garden. She carefully fed and attended the tiny worms and she taught the people of Hotan how silk was made. Soon Hotan became rich from making and selling silk.

After many years Hotan became a part of China, but not before silk-making spread to many lands. The people of Hotan can show this very day where, as legend says, the princess, whose name has been lost in the mists of time, took off her hat and gave the prince the silkworm eggs. Every year a cocoon festival is held in memory of the brave little Princess.

Sue Palmer

Deep In The Jungle

Deep in the jungle
where the lion walks,
Monkeys play
and a tiger stalks.
Carefully camouflaged
in grasses tall,
Quietly he creeps,
barely seen at all.

Elephants trumpet
trunks held high.
They walk into the river
that runs nearby.
Birds take flight,
a crocodile snaps.
"You can't eat me,"
said the hippo.
"That's a fact!"

Deep in the forest,
squirrels scamper up a tree.
A brown bear sniffs,
searching for his tea.
The deer run fast,
to get out of his way.
They won't be his dinner
at least not today.

Badgers forage
on the forest floor.
A red fox eats insects
he'd like some more.
A racoon peeps out
from a hollow in the tree.
"I think I'll catch a fish.
It's time for my tea."

Sioban Timmer

Ambling Rambles

Marching through the
Everglade, my soul
Appeased by
Dappled shade.
Enchanting breeze to
Ruffle hair
Meander on without a care.

Lynne Tatam

Fallen Trees

Groaning and shrieking the last one fell
Crashing wildly into the deep, dark dell
Ancient giants broken, bodies scattered around
Motionless and silent they lay dying on the ground

Sacrificed to progress at such a terrible cost
Land scorched and burned, whole forests lost
Woodlands stripped down into dust and sand
Once verdant and lush now a desolate land

The earth rebels at the pain we give
She decides if we die or live
Our arrogance and power cannot withstand
Mother Nature's hard and often brutal hand

The continued plunder set to seal our fate
Insanity must cease but have we left it too late?
Grieving we'll drop to our bended knees
"You will never learn," sigh the fallen trees

Barbara Gurney

Road to Nowhere

Somewhere in the mist of memory
Somewhere where my heart once lived
    A road led me to you

Amongst the fresh-faced flush of youth
Amongst a plan of a forever
    A road beckoned on

Beside flowers of paired contentment
Beside blossoms of wedded bliss
    A road turned corners

Because pain became your struggle
Because tragedy encompassed me
    A road became a detour

When my soul broke from your passing
When loneliness covered my all
    A road became less travelled

Somewhere in the mist of memory
Somewhere while my heart lives empty
    That road leads to nowhere

Pat Marshall

The Last Christmas?

Six-year-old Paul was looking forward to Christmas. He and his mum, Elizabeth, had flown from Melbourne to Perth and were staying with Paul's Nana, until the big truck, with all their furniture on it, arrived at the new house. Dad was driving from Melbourne, and due to arrive the day before the van.

Four days before Christmas Elizabeth telephoned Janet in the removalist's office to find out when the truck would be arriving at the house the next day. That was when the trouble began.

"You know the truck is coming "pick-a-back" on the train from Port Augusta to Kalgoorlie? Well, the train has been held up because the heat has distorted the rails. A diversion is being built, but it is going to take a few hours."

"But when will we get our things?" Elizabeth was worried, because most of Paul's Christmas presents were in the trailer with the household goods.

"We are hoping the truck will be in Perth late tomorrow night," Janet replied, "so we should be able to deliver for you on the twenty-third."

"Oh, well, I suppose one more day will not matter too much. I'll just have to get organised a bit more quickly. Please, will you telephone me tomorrow to let me know how things are going?"

"Yes, of course we will." And with that Elizabeth had to be content.

When Brian arrived late that afternoon Elizabeth told him of the delay.

"Never mind, love; we'll manage," was his comforting reply.

The next day, Tuesday twenty-second, the phone rang about ten thirty. Brian answered it.

"Mr Johnson, I'm afraid the news is not good. The rail diversion isn't ready, and the trailer will not reach Kalgoorlie until four am on the twenty-fourth at the earliest. Can we postpone your delivery until after Christmas?"

Elizabeth could see the look of disappointment on Brian's face.

"What's wrong?" she asked.

"They want to postpone the delivery until after Christmas."

"Let me talk to them." And Elizabeth took the telephone from her husband's hand.

"Please, it's most important we have our things by Christmas day." Elizabeth's voice broke with tears. "It could be our son Paul's last Christmas. He has leukaemia."

"Mrs Johnson, give me a few minutes and I'll call you back." Janet's voice was sympathetic. Ten minutes later the phone rang again.

"Mrs Johnson, you will have your goods, even if we have to deliver on Christmas Day! That is a firm promise."

"Thank you! Thank you, very much."

The remainder of that day, and all the next, Brian, Elizabeth and Paul spent at the new house, meeting the neighbours, weeding and watering the garden, doing what they could to get ready to receive the furniture when it arrived. They planned which item should go where, particularly the things for Paul's room. They even bought a small Christmas tree and set it up in the sitting room, but, with few presents to put underneath, it looked rather forlorn.

Late on the afternoon of twenty-third December, Janet rang from the removalist's office.

"The diversion is complete, the train is due in Kalgoorlie at eight am tomorrow. The trailer will be off-loaded as quickly as possible, but it is not likely to be in Perth until six o'clock tomorrow evening. We have to unload the things at the back of the trailer before we can reach yours. I have talked with the boss, and if you are agreeable we can deliver your goods early on Christmas morning."

"Oh yes, please!" Elizabeth was breathless with relief. "What time will it be?"

"Well, that rather depends on you. The driver and his helpers would like to make it as early as possible Would six am at the house be OK?"

"Yes, yes!" Elizabeth didn't care how early it had to be. She wanted only to get the things into the house and retrieve Paul's presents.

"Thank you, Mrs Johnson. I'll ring again tomorrow afternoon to confirm everything. By the way, does Paul still believe in Father Christmas?"

"Yes, I think so. In fact, I told him Father Christmas had promised our things for Christmas Day. Why?"

"Oh, just an idea I had. I'll ring you tomorrow," and Janet rang off.

The next afternoon, Christmas Eve, the party for the staff and their families was held at the removalist's depot. After Father Christmas, in red suit, black boots, and fluffy white wiskers, had handed out gifts to all the children, the boss explained about the early delivery the next morning, and asked for a couple more volunteers to help with the unloading. Eight of the men offered, including "Father Christmas".

Janet also said she would be there, to help Mrs Johnson, "And, Bill, wear your

Father Christmas outfit. Let's make it as memorable a day as possible for Paul and his family. I'll ring Mrs Johnson now and confirm we will be there at six am."

The neighbours on either side of the new house were surprised when Brian, Elizabeth, Paul, and both sets of grandparents arrived just before six o'clock on Christmas morning, but they were stunned when the removal truck pulled up and Father Christmas climbed out.

"Does a boy named Paul live here?" Father Christmas had a lovely mellow booming voice.

"Yes! That's me. I'm Paul," he said, jumping up and down with excitement.

"Well Paul, I've come to make sure my friends here had the right address." Father Christmas turned to the men getting out of the cars which had followed the truck down the street. "OK boys. You can start to unload. This is the right house."

Janet had equipped herself and all the helpers with floppy red Christmas hats, so it looked as if a swarm of very large pixies was at work. With Father Christmas in charge outside, Brian and Janet directing traffic inside, and Elizabeth and the grandparents busily unpacking and stowing things away, Paul could only sit and watch.

The neighbour on one side arrived with an enormous jug of fresh lemonade and a pile of plastic drinking mugs, and stayed to help. The neighbour on the other side delivered a large plate of homemade shortbread. "I'll get the plate later, when things have quietened down a little." And she was gone.

With the large number of helpers to unload the furniture, and the careful planning of where it should be put, it didn't take long for the job to be completed. Just before eight o'clock the large trailer was empty.

"There is just one more item." And Father Christmas reached into the cab of the truck. "Where is Paul?"

"Here I am!"

Father Christmas had a brightly wrapped package in his hand.

"Merry Christmas, Paul. This is a special present for a very special boy."

"Oh, thank you!" said Paul. "May I open it now?"

"Of course." And Paul quickly unwrapped a fluffy white bear, wearing a Christmas waistcoat.

"He's lovely. I shall call him Rudolph. Thank you very much." Then more shyly he continued, "Are you really Father Christmas?"

"What do you think?"

"Well, Mum said Father Christmas had promised all our things would be here for Christmas day, so I think you must be." Then he grinned. "But your beard has slipped."

Father Christmas laughed.

"Merry Christmas," he called, as he climbed into the removal van and was driven away.

"Merry Christmas," called the pixie helpers as their cars followed the van down the street.

"Merry Christmas, Paul!" Janet removed her pixie hat and placed it on Paul's head. She waved as she too drove after the van.

"Merry Christmas," echoed Brian and Elizabeth, "and thank you. Thank you so much."

"I wonder if people will believe me when I tell them all our furniture was delivered on Christmas Day by Father Christmas," Paul said. Hugging his new bear, he ran into the house. "Mum, Dad, can we open some more presents?"

Elizabeth laughed at Paul's enthusiasm. She looked at the little tree, now surrounded by brightly wrapped packages.

"Let's have some breakfast first, love, then we can spend the rest of the day opening presents!"

Bernie Williams

The Star

Last night I looked up at the stars
The rocking lulled me into a trance
The sky went back
Not a single light
A total void
Then one single star
One single light
The warm golden rays
Drew me into your heart
My own heart melted and
Fused into yours
I knew your
Gentleness
Compassion
Caring
Empathy
I knew your soul.

I am not the same
I can't separate
What has been fused together
Can't hide from your soul
Can never deny your love
Or the love I have for my Star.

Lavender Tapestries

Look, come see, come see.
Red and purple tapestries
grace the fertile fields.

Fields stretch before me.
Rich, red earth and lavender.
Misty mauve vistas.

Freshly harvested,
Lavender yields her treasures.
Posies, perfume, oil.

Carolyn Nelson

Number One, Acacia Drive

The old house looked warm and peaceful as the car pulled up outside,
But the driver had a purpose which would not reflect with pride.
He smiled and rubbed his hands with glee, thinking of what it was worth,
With no conscience for the lady who had cared for him since birth.
All his plans led to this moment and this was his pay-off day,
He knew with charm or bullying he was sure to get his way.
There could be no thought of failure as the odds of that were slim,
With some heavy-handed treatment she would sign the house to him.
His hand patted his breast pocket, the commitment papers signed,
He had really been convincing proving she had lost her mind.
The paper authorised a bed in a care facility
Owned by gullible do-gooders of a local charity.
He allowed himself five minutes to sift through his memories
To enhance the glowing picture of the life he'd live at ease.
She had been his only parent but he never called her Mum,
They had not been raised Church-goers, even though she had been one.
Every Sunday, she had dressed up and had waited by the gate,
A car arrived at nine am which had never turned up late.
She always said, "I'm off to Church" and would be gone for the day,
Meanwhile he and his three brothers had remained at home to play.
In the charge of her house-keeper, there had been fun things to do,
Mrs Watts said they were lucky they were not Church-goers too!
The lady ... he called Gwendolyn, prim and proper ... so well bred,
Wasn't really their own mother, just someone their Dad had wed.
After marriage he had walked out leaving her to raise his sons,
He always thought she was a fool to take on such hellions.
Two had died in the armed forces and the third one fighting drugs,
"A policeman" said with such contempt ... all his brothers had been mugs.

He laughed, said, "I'm the clever one, her whole fortune will be mine
Through the Power of Attorney papers I will make her sign."
Then impatience overwhelmed him, it was time to get it done,
Said, imagining the outcome, "This is going to be fun."
The gate swung in without a sound and he preened with ownership,
As nothing had been overlooked and success was in his grip.
He marched up to the fly-screen door but the handle wouldn't turn,
He had to ring the antique bell and his rage began to burn.
Her footsteps echoed on the tiles then the door was opened wide
And the burn became a simmer as she welcomed him inside.
"Hello Rick," ... so pleased to see him as she sat to serve him tea,
He smiled, delighting in the thought of how easy this would be.
She was chatting about something but he didn't take it in,
He was thinking of his options and the best way to begin.
He chose charm and feigned affection as her last surviving son,
Simply caring for his mother as his brothers would have done.
There was silence for a moment, she expected a reply,
He had missed some foolish comment that his musing let slip by.
He decided to ignore it and he laid the papers out,
She would picture his devotion with no element of doubt.
"I consider it my duty, and your welfare is supreme."
He recited ... words well practised ... "And we're family ... A team."
"You need only sign these papers and your worries will be through
That way I repay the kindness I have always had from you."
"I will take on all your burdens," spoken in a caring tone,
"This house is much too big for you to be managing alone."
He smiled and handed her the pen which would alter both their lives,
Then he fired his last volley, "I'm the last son who survives."
She was calm and softly-spoken when she told him, "This won't do,
I've never owned this lovely house so I can't give it to you."
"It belongs to my ex-husband and his wealthy family,
In my settlement agreement they let me live here, cost free."
"You will not receive a penny, not at this or any stage."
The words had turned his plans to dust and he flew into a rage.
He was just about to strike her when a strong hand grabbed his fist
And bent his arm behind his back with a force few could resist.
Felt the coldness of the metal as the handcuffs clicked in place,
Then recoiled in abject terror when he saw ... his brother's face!
The shock had held him paralysed, though his throat wanted to yell,

Was forced to sit, as Simon said, "You had better listen well."
"I've been working undercover, only Mum has known the truth,
  I could not cause her to worry as I did throughout my youth."
"You can put away your scheming, your cajoling and your threats,
  All that you've got coming to you is what heartlessness begets."
"Now you'll sit here and you'll listen to our Mother's history
  Or I'll throw your ass in prison for your vile duplicity."
  Simon said, "You need to tell him," and he stood beside her chair,
  Reassuring with his presence as he gently smoothed her hair.
"I was raised by my grandparents," Gwendolyn said quietly,
"And their main consideration was providing care for me."
"They arranged for me to marry, when their health was in decline,
  A man obsessed with furthering his perceived dynastic line."
"We married and they passed away but all kindness he reserved,
  Once I birthed my son and daughter, he had thought my purpose served."
"Without family to back me, I had lacked the funds to fight
  When evicted into this life, out of my young children's sight."
"It was only for appearance that he cared for me at all,
  But he let me see my children, a concession somewhat small."
"He allowed one weekly visit, a four hour drive away,
  Where, for only thirty minutes I could see my children play."
"I could watch ... but make no contact and most times it made me cry,
  But I felt a hope ... a promise ... when I'd catch my daughter's eye."
At those words, a woman walked in with a baby in her arms,
"I'm Max," and Gwendolyn just beamed, as if they were lucky charms.
  She said, "I am your brother's wife and my mother's youngest child,
  No harm will ever come to her now that we are reconciled."
"Both my father and my brother were unfeeling and unkind,
  They forbade talk of my mother and to this I was resigned."
"Then I met your older brother, he was like a magic link,
  He freed me of their tyranny and their life lived on the brink."
"He provided a connection to a mother, seldom seen,
  Who, (my father had insisted), I remembered from a dream."
"Now we live that dream together and build new dreams every day,
  Since my father and my brother freed us, when they went away."
As she studied Rick's expression, her grey eyes showed her unease,
"How could you and he be brothers, when you feel like a disease?"
"Of a home, you're undeserving, even less of family,
  I would cast you to the gutter if the choice were up to me."

"But the choice must be my mother's, who I'm sure feels no surprise
At your plan to make her homeless, being used to all your lies."
"So we're rich now," Rick responded, "and as you're my brother's wife
I will still get what I wanted, I will have my easy life."
With a voice quite unrepentant said, "It all worked out somehow,
Just as it always does for me ... You can take the cuffs off now."
And the silence that descended came with shock and disbelief,
But not for his elder brother who knew him to be a thief.
"You mistake your lucky fortune, how do you believe we met?
I was working undercover on a drug case ... you forget!"
"Both the men have been convicted and can't profit from their crime."
But then Max had interrupted, "Let me make it clear this time."
"Their great wealth was confiscated, all but this one property,
As Number One, Acacia Drive, did and does, belong to me."
But Rick couldn't be discouraged, he said "There's a stash somewhere,
You want to keep it for yourselves but I mean to get my share."
All hope his brother might reform had been dashed by those few words
And Simon saw the same contempt he had seen on most jailbirds.
"You didn't hear a single word, you just saw the dollar sign,
Perhaps the only way you'll learn is the hard way ... serving time."
Then he gathered up the papers and he called his partner in,
With the evidence presented, he said stoically ... "Charge him!"

Sue Palmer

Gathering Moments

I take a sip of hot, steaming tea. It tastes good, inviting me to take another. My thoughts drift to how often I have a cup of tea while combining tasks—on the run, always busy. But, not this morning I decide, I pick up my cup, determined to pause and enjoy it fully. Walking outside onto the patio I step down onto the lawn noting grey skies overhead. There has been a light shower of rain.

Listening, I hear the twittering of little birds in shrubs nearby. They chase each other, darting in and out of the branches, dive bombing, pausing occasionally to fluff up their feathers. They are enjoying their morning shower as they fly through leafy wetness.

Touching my face, I feel cool, damp skin, so too my hair. There is a slight chill in the air, my hands close around the warmth of the liquid in my cup. I am being bathed in the finest rain, a soft curtain of gossamer mist. Closing my eyes I stand and allow myself to take in this sensory experience. I think to myself, "Is this living in the moment?"

The mist turns to drizzle; I feel the rain on my face and running down my bare arms, life-giving, life-sustaining rain. Raindrops plop into my cup and I walk up the steps back under the shelter of the patio roof. Choosing a comfy chair, I sit back with outstretched legs slowly sipping my cup of tea. Consciously, I allow my body to relax, sinking into the soft cushions. I close my eyes, ears tuned to the gentle sound of falling rain. The sound is pleasant, soothing, bringing calmness to my soul. I wonder, "Surely this is living in the moment."

Rain begins to fall very heavily now, an acoustic drumming on the roof. Thunder rolls in the distance and lightening cracks, the elements are having a nature party all of their own. I can almost hear my garden sighing with gratefulness. This heavy, soaking rain will reach thirsty roots deep in the soil. I watch as the steps turn into a waterfall, water cascading from one level to the next and onto lawn that is happy to receive it.

The birdbath is full and water flows over the sides. I hear the sound of water gushing through the downpipes and hope that the gutters are not blocked. Looking up, I watch as droplets of water chase one another along the edge dripping to the earth below. The refreshing odour of wet grass and soil carried on the wind reaches my nose. "Ah, living in the moment," I whisper softly.

The rain finally eases and I rise from my chair walking to the edge of the patio. I catch my breath as the rotary clothes hoist captures my attention, my focus is not really on the structure itself but on the beauty of the symmetry it hosts. It looks like a see-through umbrella with spines covered in a watery web of beads.

The sun valiantly endeavours to peep from behind her shroud. I watch mesmerized as a rainbow begins to emerge, my water beads have turned into glistening diamonds. The rainbow now has a reflection, two bows of brilliant colour arching across the heavens. I wonder, wouldn't it be fun to take a stroll across them? What a delight it would be to slide down this glorious profusion of colour! Now that would be a truly momentous occasion.

I think to myself, I am blessed, what a busy morning I've had, of experiences, wonderings and imaginings. I'll gather each of these special moments and pop them into the storehouse of my memory. Picking up my cup, I rise and walk back into the house; it must be time to put the kettle on.

Lynne Tatam

Horror Story Fashion House

We arrived at the castle lit by cold moonlight
The invitation foretold of an unforgettable night
Slowly our eyes adjusted to the soft misty gloom
We were stunned into silence by the vast ballroom

Three hundred guests were seated, all a-twitter
Gazing speechless at the glam rock glitter
Music blared out, a giant spotlight beamed down
A single model posed in a posh designer gown

She strutted and shimmied then spun right around
Our collective jaws rattled as they hit the ground
Her queenly gaze scanned the assembled crowd
Gasps of amazement were uttered out loud

Violet skinned Megona, a goddess ten foot high
In the center of her forehead sat a single golden eye
Royally she waved at the open-mouthed throng
Then completely vanished as the next sashayed on

Beautiful Skulla entered, draped in fine black lace
A seductive smile hovered on the white rictus face
Pearly bones gleamed and clattered in the dark
Her being shone redly from an eerie inner spark

The catwalk was on fire as each creation appeared
No longer a spectacle to be hated, judged or feared
"Thank you," said the M.C. in a low, silken voice
"For attending this evening and staying quite by choice"

"In our world acceptance is very rarely found
Yet, you considered normal quickly rallied around
Horror Story Fashion House its path now crystal clear
Invites you to our next soiree, in the coming year."

One by one on they blazed beaming at the crowd
Followed by thunderous applause, deafeningly loud
Champagne flowed endlessly drunk with thirsty glee
The in crowd partied hard and long - it was THE place to be

All too soon a tolling bell forecast the coming dawn
Our friendly souls of the night feared the light of morn
Halloween night faded into all hallows day
The gentle dead amongst us quietly slipped away

Terry Duhig

Being Bugs

"Love at first sight" could not be the words recalled when I first laid eyes on my gorgeous wife Claire, and she, without any doubt, would say the same about her first viewing of me.

Any deliberate casting back causes my brain's computer to delve into a dark corner where a file with the title of "Ridiculous horror" is stored.

Her memory file of that same moment, and guessing that she also has one, would be more than likely titled "Hilarious and almost unbelievable".

With the aim of boosting the amount of pocket money for a booked holiday to Bali, I responded to a Party Entertainment Agency's advert for dressed up greeting singers. On my first, and as it turned out, my only engagement, I appeared in a Bugs Bunny costume at a private lunchtime birthday party on the outskirts of Mundijong.

The rehearsed act took me no more than three minutes to perform and it was well received. I left shortly afterwards and it was my intention to change back into my everyday clothing once I returned to my car, however the weather forecast of a cloudy and mainly fine day was at its unpredictable best.

Leaving the house, it would have been no more than thirty metres to where my old Datsun was parked beyond some trees, this distance had been requested to ensure my visit would be a surprise for the Birthday Girl. It was raining, no not raining, it was pouring.

I ran. Bugs Bunny still had his head attached. My vision was affected.

I know this is a silly question, but have you ever tried to run fast in a Bugs Bunny suit? If you have then you'd know that the loose and baggy cloth around your socks would have you stumbling and staggering. This was me doing that exactly, and just short of those trees I fell, and you guessed it, I splash-landed into mud, face first.

Unluckily, before I ventured out into the open, I had the sense to retrieve my car ignition key which I had on a chain from around my neck, and was holding it in my left paw, the one that had my hand inside, the same paw that I thrust forward, automatically, as I fell.

When I slipped and slopped and pushed my way up to be in standing position once again, a wide opened left paw showed it no longer held the key.

My reaction may be forgiven by understanding folk, for it caused me to loudly utter a word. A word which would have been totally unsuitable for saying some minutes earlier.

The storm, for that what it was, moved solidly above me, heavy black clouds made the afternoon appear almost as if it was night. The rain fell hard and fast, and as I looked down, I could see that as the rain struck the mud, it caused it to splash upwards. I prayed to Zeus, the God of rain, asking forgiveness for my profanity, for a miracle to occur and for a small key to be washed back to the surface by the force of the pounding water. Well, not really, but I did think about it for a couple of seconds; then I bent down and started scooping up mud around where I guessed my paw had landed. My guessing was way out. I must have stumbled forward a couple of steps regaining my balance. Pawing, rabbit style into mud was a total and utter failure, but as I was about to surrender to my hopeless position, Zeus must have read my brief thought, for above my bent and soaking wet frame, the clouds suddenly parted and a beam of sunlight was allowed to shine down. A miracle occurred. A fraction of metal glittered in the oozing slush just inches below my Bunny Costume Nose.

I was saved, but only for that unique moment as more frustration awaited yours truly.

Feeling like an almost drowned rabbit; you'd know how that is, wouldn't you? Or would you?

No matter. I felt a little easier once I had removed Bugsy's head from off my shoulders.

Several sheets of a Saturday newspaper lined my car seat, these to soak up the flowing waters from my still dripping outfit. I had made the decision that it would be better for me to drive back to my home and have a hot shower before dressing once more in my everyday clothes. With a bit of luck, I would be back in Gosnells within, say, twenty minutes, all being well.

Did I just think that all would be well? Yuck, I was completely wrong again. Instead of heading for the South West Highway, I rashly, in the still pouring rain, turned into a narrow bitumen road, crazily thinking, and I don't, for the life of me, know why, that it appeared to be heading in the same direction as the Highway, and it would be quieter and hopefully get me into Byford that much sooner, from there I would then go on to the highway. Should have made contact with Zeus again.

Within a couple of kilometres the bitumen ceased and I was lurching along a gravel stretch with no obvious place to turn around, so I continued to have the tyres crunch their way along a mixture of limestone and mainly small rocks; of which there was the odd larger variety which lurched the Datsun up and down, and at the same time, my backside repeatedly left and then fell back on to the now wet, sticky newspaper. I was hoping the unmade section wouldn't go on for too long. My hope came true, it didn't.

To my delight I espied bitumen once more, and a good feeling encouraged my accelerator foot to press down that much harder.

You know the wise old saying, "more haste, less speed", yeah, I later remembered that too.

I moved on to the sealed road, just about twenty metres, no more for sure, then a rapid bump after bump had the front of the car aiming for the side of that narrow road with its banked up dirt and a wired fence beyond; at the same time, the steering wheel was trying ferociously to slide out of my gripping paws. I knew precisely what had happened, my nearside tyre had blown.

Fighting back on the steering and gently braking, I was successful in stopping with the whole car having bitumen still beneath it.

You know how that on rare occasions, one gets the feeling one is not going to have a good day; well, I now had that feeling. Strange isn't it?

Getting out, I put Bugsy's head back on, still pouring that wet stuff, and then studied the front nearside tyre, noting it was only flat on the bottom part was depressing enough, but a sudden realisation caused doom to add a darker shadow over me; and it wasn't the fact it was still raining, and that I had Bugsy's head back on my shoulders, it was another flat tyre.

It was my brother's flat tyre. The one he had on his car last Friday. He had borrowed my jack so he could put his spare tyre on, and promised to return the jack before the weekend.

He didn't.

Thunder claps and lightning flashes were happening every minute or so. Zeus was presumably no longer interested in my predicament. I was defeated and felt like sobbing, however the thought of crying inside the extra head I was wearing was cancelled.

I knew I wouldn't be able to wipe tears away with my paws, so I stared at the road ahead, then at the wire fence and beyond it, only because I didn't know what else to do.

I was wrong about Zeus, so wrong; he had taken pity on me. As I stared, his next lightning flashed, and beyond the fence, it lit up the outline of a house.

I became energized and peered through interfering rain, and what I saw made me smile; on my face that is, not the Rabbit's head. There were faintly glowing lights in what I guessed to be the house windows. Good old Zeus, he came good for me once again.

Sloshing my way ahead, I searched for the driveway off the road which led to the house. I still wasn't coping too well trying to stride out with floppy paws on my soaked socks, and not achieving immediate success at seeing either a gate or an open driveway.

I was deciding whether to keep going on the way in front of me or turn around and try the opposite direction. Three skinny-trunked trees further forward were hindering my view, get as far as them and that would be far enough I thought.

Good thinking. I smiled once more; those bits of timber had hidden a sign which had words "Lot 245 Stevenson". Next to it was a hard crossover in front of an opened gate and an enticing gravel driveway. I took a couple of deep breaths and left the road.

The rough surface was not at all pleasing for my feet, but my determination to cover the ground to the house overpowered any desire to stop. The size of the house was increasing with every step, and I was still smiling, but I didn't reach it, not immediately anyhow.

In front of and to its right was a garage, its doors were open, and inside I could see the tail of a utility. I heard the sound of banging, and I could also make out, under the glow of a light, its bonnet. I turned, moved forward until I stood just inside that opening, out of the rain. Waiting for a few seconds, I loudly called out, "Hello, hello, anyone there?"

A shuffling noise brought a figure into view, a torch was lifted to shine its beam right on me and that made it harder to gain a clearer vision than my initial sighting, which lasted no more than a second. I still managed to make out a person in overalls and what seemed to be a beanie pulled down as far as the eyes and I knew they were staring at me.

"What the ... What the heck are you?" A female voice asked.

"Hello, I've got a flat," I answered.

"A what?" This was half gasped and half blurted back at me.

"A flat, out there." I waved an arm held paw back towards the road.

A giggle started, then it was abruptly silenced, and the voice added, "Is that what you call it, I've always thought that bunnies came out of holes in the ground, and by the look of you it was a pretty muddy one that you've crawled out of."

"No, you don't understand, I've got a flat and need help," I desperately pleaded.

"Uh! ... Hold on ... Are you asking me to come to your flat and nibble a carrot with you?"

She, I thought, was now having a bit of fun with me, and taking the Mickey.

I lost it. I jerked Bugsy's head off my shoulders and raised my voice—just a few decibels. "I have a rotten, stinking flat tyre out there on my car. I'm soaking wet, fed up, because I don't have a jack, and I'm stuck in this Bunny suit." I then lowered my voice back to the pleading tone, "Please, I really would like some help."

All the time we had this stretched out conversation the torchlight was aimed at me.

It was now lowered. She pulled the beanie from her head and long auburn curly hair fell down to her neck. She was still staring at me, seemingly deep in thought.

"Right!" she exclaimed, and then turning to a small opened window, she hollered, "Dad! I've got an oversized bunny here in the garage, could do with some help."

"A bunny?" a male voice queried, then it firmed and quickly added, "Don't scare it, be right with you."

She looked back at me and smiled, a nice friendly smile, and informed me, "My Dad, he'll be here in a minute."

Actually it was only about thirty seconds later that a side door swung open, and its frame filled by a tall, solidly-built man. That was a brief description. I really did not take that much of a look at him, my concentration was on the double-barrelled shotgun he was raising upwards.

I instinctively dived to my left and my bunny covered body thumped heavily onto the concrete floor. Bugsy's head was no longer held and it flew away. I was terrified.

"No, Dad! Put it down, this one is tame," the female shouted.

The next morning, being Sunday, I was up early and washed and polished my Datsun, the one with the four, well pumped-up, wheels. The flat I dropped off for repair at a Byford garage and I arranged to collect it the following day, before continuing on my way to Lot 245 on the back road to Mundijong.

That was successfully achieved, and whilst in Byford, at the tavern, I bought a sixpack of Fosters to go with the bunch of flowers, these as a thanks-a-lot to Mr and Mrs Stevenson, who had warmed me up with hot coffee, and where, after using their shower, I changed into my normal clothing.

Once that storm had disappeared over the hills and took its rain with it, Dad Stevenson, in no time at all, had my flat off and the spare on in its place, he was ably assisted by Claire, their eldest daughter, who, now out of her overalls and in a dress, looked just great.

She and I went out the following Friday to the Armadale Cinema, with a dinner afterwards.

That was the start of us going out on a regular basis, and by the end of the year we were making plans to be married.

When I took the outfit back to the Agency, they weren't pleased at all with the state of it, they reckoned it was ruined, so I offered to buy it; in the end we agreed they give it to me instead of paying me for the party engagement.

It's extra large, so if anyone would like to hire it from me, I can be approached with a reasonable offer.

All that was a couple of years ago, and nowadays, whenever I look back at being Bugs Bunny, I don't think it was so bad after all. I often put it on for a laugh nowadays. I tell friends it's just an amusement, y'know, it's a plaything.

The Cobblers
A Modern Fairy Tale

"Do you have the photos of the models, Linda?" Ray asked.

"Right here," Linda replied.

"Then bring in the designers," Ray instructed.

Linda opened the door and beckoned Brad, Paul and John to come in.

"I have employed the services of three experienced models, they are all extremely beautiful and are used to only the best," Ray said.

How pompous Ray is, thought Linda.

"The first task of your internship is to design a pair of shoes for your model," Ray continued. "You will each take a photograph unseen from Linda, and get started. I expect to see shoes that are innovative, beautiful and reflect your abilities. The models will wear the shoes you have made, from when they wake up next Thursday, until they arrive here wearing your shoes at three pm. You have five days, so get busy."

Brad stepped forward first, wanting to get the best looking girl, but Linda held the photos face down, so he picked the middle photograph, hoping for the best. Linda walked across to the other designers, and held out the remaining two pictures. She wanted John to get a picture he could work with. He seemed a nice guy, the only one who had bothered to find out her full name. She'd already seen the pictures and though all three seemed intimidating to the retiring little secretary, one did seem slightly less so than the other two. Paul however took first choice, and John took the last picture with a smile, and the first "Thank you" Linda had heard that day.

Ray returned to his office, and looked at his calendar, Friday the thirteenth, not a good omen. Then he took a double take. Friday the thirteenth of September, his birthday. Flo had asked him at breakfast if he had any plans for the day, and he told her he was arranging a competition for the interns. She hadn't responded. Well she'd probably forgotten his birthday, or perhaps she was punishing him for

123

forgetting hers. Either way he didn't have time to worry, not with the factory being in crisis. All my skills seem to have disappeared, Ray reflected. If these three don't come up with some solutions, I'm not sure what I'll do.

The interns shuffled into the workroom, deep in thought. All three looked at their photograph. On the bottom right was a sticker naming the model, her height and shoe size.

Brad thought he'd seen his model in a catalogue or maybe in the press. She's gorgeous, he thought. Perhaps I'll ask her for a date. I'll hire a Merc. She's tall. Lucky I'm tall. Maybe they're all tall. Poor old John probably won't reach his model's shoulder. Genelle, a classy name for a stunning girl. I'll design the sexiest shoes in the world for you, Genelle.

Paul too thought he had a great model. Her name's Roberta, I'll Google and see if I can find out about her likes and dislikes. Paul found endless pictures of Roberta and a short biography. He breathed a sigh of relief when he saw that sport was amongst her list of likes. Paul lived for sport and he liked to win. He thought, with Roberta he could. He also noticed that neither of the other designers seemed interested in finding out anything about the girls who would wear their shoes. Yes, thought Paul, I'm in with a good chance.

John didn't do more than glance at the picture of his model. He noted her name was Stephanie and memorised her shoe size. He already knew what he wanted to do.

The designers worked tirelessly, and on Wednesday evening three pairs of shoes were delivered to the modelling agency and handed over to the models.

Thursday seemed endless to Brad and Paul, but John remained calm and collected, making coffee for everyone, joking and chatting to relieve the tension.

At quarter to three Linda once again beckoned the designers in.

At three Ray announced he'd present the models in the order in which they had been chosen, the designers would explain their creative thoughts and each model would give her opinion on her shoes.

Genelle was first. Wow, I've done it, thought Brad. She's as tall as I am on those heels. I wish she'd worn something a bit more glitzy, but she is so hot. Then he flushed as he realised he should have been explaining his design.

"My design makes Genelle the woman of every man's dreams," he began. "I chose red, with diamond heels to make every head turn. The styling is innovative in that the shoe looks as though it is held together by air. No one could make a shoe more glamorous than this."

"Genelle?" said Ray.

"This is the worst shoe I have ever forced my foot into," complained Genelle. "My little girl burst into tears when she saw me this morning, and I fell over the step at the day care. My calves ache and my feet feel as though they're set in concrete. I would never buy a shoe like this nor would anyone I know in the real world."

"Thank you, Genelle," said Ray.

But Genelle didn't respond from the floor where she was trying to prise the shoes from her feet, while muttering quite audible modern expletives.

Linda helped Genelle to a chair while Ray went to fetch Roberta.

Paul thought Roberta looked great in her gym clothes. She wore a helmet, and seemed more than competent at using her footwear.

"My shoes show style, but more than anything they show innovation," announced Paul. "As you can see each shoe has ancillary functions which allow the wearer to win almost any competitive event she enters. They give women the edge they deserve to excel at any physical challenge presented."

"Roberta?" said Ray

"Well it was fun for a while giving a can of whip ass," laughed Roberta, "but I wouldn't buy these shoes. I think these are cheating shoes, and I like to feel I have a reputation as a good friend and a good sport. Also I feel exhausted living at the pace these shoes demand."

Roberta made her own way to a chair and Ray went to fetch Stephanie.

Linda was pleased when Stephanie walked into the room, she had hoped John would get this model and Stephanie looked even more approachable in the flesh than she had in the photo.

"Hello, Stephanie," said John. "I'm John, and I'm happy to let you talk about my shoes."

Ray looked disapproving, but merely said, "Stephanie?"

"Well," said Stephanie. "These shoes are stylish, comfortable, and probably innovative though I don't know quite what that means. But ... sorry, John, but these shoes aren't really me. I don't know if it's because they're grey, or maybe just not my style. They are comfortable though, I might even buy them, I just don't love them."

John stood up and looked as though he would like to give Stephanie a hug, but thought better of it as he realised he would land up with his face in her boobs, so instead patted her arm comfortingly.

"Quite right," he soothed. "Very perceptive of you, Stephanie."

John knelt down and retrieved a second pair of identical but far smaller shoes from his bag. Turning to Linda he said, "Would you do me the honour of modelling my shoes, Linda-ella?"

Linda's cheeks turned pink as John slipped on the shoes.

Linda has amazing blue eyes, thought Brad

Linda has an athletic figure for such a small girl, thought Paul.

Linda is looking at John like Flo used to look at me, thought Ray.

Genelle, Roberta, and Stephanie gathered round Linda-ella telling her how beautiful she looked and how perfect the shoes were for her.

Linda felt like a million dollars.

This is a fairy tale, and we all know fairy tales end with a couple falling in love, moving in together, having a baby, then a picture perfect wedding and of course fantastic sex for ever after, and for John and Linda-ella that is what happened. But this is a modern inclusive fairy tale so it isn't exactly all that happened.

Ray and John formed a partnership, and Ray got his mojo back by designing a pair of shoes exactly right for Flo.

Linda-ella and Flo White became BFF, even producing their first offspring within two days of each other at the same hospital.

Ray and John found out even perfect shoes wear out and pregnancy and motherhood necessitate a lot of adjustment in the footwear department.

Brad and Paul became part of the Factories Dream Team, which was featured in two series on reality T.V.

Brad bought a Mercedes but found to his horror, he was happier driving a Jeep. After being caught on camera wearing the glamorous high heels he loved to design, he found a lucrative niche market in the world of cross dressing.

Paul became addicted to the canteen's sticky buns. He found a significant other in the canteen lady who said she loved him because he was so well-rounded. He was admired by millions for designing perfect slippers.

The Dream Team's slogan *You don't need every pair of shoes in the world, just the one that's right for you,* became a catch phrase worldwide.

As for the models:

Genelle wrote a book full of complaints, peppered with modern expletives, titled *These Boots are Made for Kickin-ass.* It became a handbook for the modern feminist movement.

Roberta continued with her studies and worked as a human rights lawyer.

Stephanie honed her skills at empathy while keeping a clear view of her own best interests and went into politics.

So eventually in their own way they did all live happily ever after.

Sue Palmer

Charlie's Song

Walking through the forest
in the summer breeze.
Koalas climbing higher
swaying in the trees.

Oh-oh what a beautiful day,
Oh-oh we've come to play.
Possums in the tree tops fast asleep.
Here on the forest floor we gently creep.

Building cubby-houses,
a bridge across the stream.
Clouds drifting overhead,
I love to lay and dream.

Oh-oh what a beautiful day,
Oh-oh we came to play.
Possums in the tree tops begin to wake.
I think it's time to go home,
Mum said, "Don't be late."

Genevieve Leslie

Count On You

Can I count on you?
To make my dreams
Come true
To love me and cherish me
And sometimes, to just
Make me feel better

Can I depend on you?
When my World's falling
Apart and darkness
Prevails,
To help me
Set sail to a better place

Can I rely on you?
When things don't make
Sense, when I have
Two pence and a whole lot
Of hope

Will you be the One?
To shine a light
On my life,
To help me make it
Through

Oh, how I've loved
And adored you
These dreams,
My hopes, and
Expectations

Sometimes I think
You may fail, in my
Perfect picture
I quiver with fear
"My dear,
Can I count on you?"
You're asking me, too.

Barbara Walton

A Rite of Passage for William

William was busily weeding the garden when the postman stopped at their letterbox and beeped his horn. Taking a pile of rather official envelopes from the postman with his own rather grimy hands, William's heart leapt as he recognised the handwriting on a small, pretty-coloured envelope that was tucked in between the larger white and buff-coloured ones.

"Well, I'll be blowed! This looks as if it's from my long-lost friend Sarah. I wonder why on earth she is writing to me after all this time. After at least two years of complete silence between us since she left town, I am really curious as to why she is getting in touch now."

Plonking himself on the garden seat he'd so often shared with Sarah as they'd pondered the meaning of life, he hastily tore open the sweet-scented pink envelope that seemed so typical of Sarah's whole nature.

"What a complete surprise!" he muttered to himself as he looked at the invitation he now held in his hand.

His thoughts wandered back to six years ago, when Sarah had first moved into their small community, to their inevitable—and for him, unforgettable - first meeting. In such a little township, you got to meet and befriend every person who came to live there.

During the four years that followed, William and Sarah had formed quite a bond because they seemed to have several interests in common. These included sport, education, social activities and they'd spent many enjoyable hours of their spare time together. It wasn't long before they began to talk about future hopes, aspirations and dreams—without him at that time having a clue that he would share no part in hers.

"So what did happen?" feeling a little sad, William asked himself. "Why did she and her family just suddenly disappear into thin air two years ago this week? I know it is exactly two years because it happened on my birthday which I will be celebrating again on this coming Friday."

129

He recalled that sad night quite clearly. He'd planned a small party for his friends and although invited, Sarah simply didn't turn up! She didn't phone, didn't text or contact him at all! That there was a mystery about her family's disappearance he had no doubt—he'd heard whispers but no distinct reasons were ever given to him. His thoughts ran on, "I've heard not a word since—from my parents or from her—until today when she hits me with this surprise!"

William re-read the words on the brief note written on beautifully perfumed paper. It was an invitation to Sarah Jane's engagement to some dude named Monty that of course he'd never heard of AND it was to be held a million light-years away—in a small town in Alberta, Canada.

Ah! he thought, his mind racing on. So that was where her family had hastily moved to when they disappeared in the dead of night from here! All the young lad knew was that they'd just vanished—apparently along with a huge amount of money her father had embezzled from the bank branch at which he'd worked since the family's arrival in town.

Of course, looking at the invitation he'd made a bit grimy with his soiled hands, he realised that of course Sarah might be preparing to get married, as he suddenly realised that she was so much older than he and most definitely in that older age bracket now.

But that age difference hadn't mattered to William during the times he'd spent with her as he'd always kind of thought that they were the same age and were on the same page—the same wavelength! Sarah had appeared happy enough to be sharing time with him then, frequently calling him her "Dear Sweet William".

Just then, the door from the house into the front garden opened and his mother walked over to him to collect the mail she could see scattered on the garden seat.

"Oh, William, you have received a letter too. Who's it from, my dear?" A smile had begun to light up her kindly face as she came closer to him.

"Oh, Mum, it's just an invitation to an engagement party but it is in Alberta, Canada, so I guess I'll have to give it a miss!"

He handed the invitation to his mother to peruse. Her face reflected bewilderment at an invitation for her son to go to Canada of all places. He sat there silently as she read the letter's contents.

"Oh Wills, so Canada's where the Spencer family fled to then? This town is better off without the lot of them; our family too because her father really duped your bank manager father; your dad really had a lot to answer for from his superiors in the bank's head office, but you were never told of this because you were so upset that Sarah had left without saying goodbye to you."

His mother spoke kindly and softly to him. She continued, "Darling, I know that Sarah was a sweet girl and a good friend of yours whilst they were living here but she is twenty years of age and a young adult now. She obviously still recalls the flatteringly huge crush you had on her when met; you were a mere ten years of age to her fourteen. All I can say to this invitation six years later is that she was kind to you whilst she lived here, but you'll have to express your response with, 'Okay, it was very kind of you Sarah but because I am turning sixteen years of age on Friday and also because Canada is a long way from Australia, I'll have to say Pass in regard to your so unexpected invitation.' But you need to add that course you wish Sarah and her fiancé Monty lots of happiness. One must do the right thing. After all, Sarah didn't commit any crime."

His mother carried on, "William, you are growing up fast and you really need to concentrate on prioritising your thoughts towards your next important year of secondary college; you've made lots of new friends already and will no doubt make many more lasting friendships throughout your life ..."

William burst in to have the last word on the subject of Sarah. "Of course, Mum, I know I had an enormous crush on Sarah and I've finally realised that although she liked me, she really saw me as a young and likeable boy with whom to share HER dreams and HER goals in life.

"During these past two years, I have definitely learnt to appreciate Sarah's and my four years of discussions about many subjects about which I was then largely unaware. She was very special to me, an integral part of my growing up and I will never forget her. So, tomorrow I'll send her a nice engagement card by return mail and include a big kiss or two from her Sweet almost-grown-up William!"

Last Will And Testament

I will not write another verse
Or live this life, eternal curse
I will not walk along the sands
Or scoop up the ocean in my hands
I will not draw another picture
Or read a piece of literature
I will not love another heart
I don't ever want to be apart
I'm going to walk a lonely path
Dark and cold
Nothing left for me to hold
No longer wish to grow old
My only wish is that those I've known
Will think of me gently and not alone
I close my eyes and drift away
No more pain but at peace by the end of this day.

Lynne Tatam

A Freo Christmas

Roaring in fiercely, gusty blasts from the sea
Rattling delicate glass baubles hanging on the tree
Peppermint gums swaying, sweetly scenting the air
The sea breeze torturing our newly styled hair

Excited children ran amok laughing and squealing
Mountains of juicy prawns plump and ready for peeling
Frosty amber beers cradled in hot slick hands
Distant waves crashing onto sun-baked sands

The call rang out, "C'mon everyone, grubs up, time to eat!"
"Kids! Wash your hands properly—before grabbing a seat."
An enormous, golden turkey sat moistly before our eyes
Flanked by mounds of vegies, salads and mince pies

The brandied Christmas pudding was duly set alight
Vivid blue flames dancing, much to our delight
Tantalizingly fruity, the warm scent hung around
Dessert was hoed into, not one child made a sound

We ate without taking breath until we could eat no more
Radiant faces happy and tummies slightly sore
We left the laden table groaning and replete
Another happy Christmas day in our old Freo Street

Sioban Timmer

The Wild Winds

This memory is a hurricane
And like the wild winds when they blow
It has no form but still shakes and knocks and slams.
Powerful, invisible and turbulent
Something I cannot control or change, but won't accept.

But even the wildest wind
Can't blow forever
Eventually it loses power, becomes the soft breeze
That gently stirs and rocks and swings.
Revisited events become accepted history
When we learn to move the way the wind blows.

Graham Bartley-Smith

Could This Have Been The First Men's Shed?

The Land Rover could go no further on the rough road which terminated at a flimsy footbridge decked with bamboo matting. Three Australians on Christmas leave, shouldered their packs and crossed the shaky structure to follow a well-defined track. A Papuan boy appeared from the high roadside grass and assured us that he would watch the vehicle. He would sleep in the car and run to his village for food.

Our destination was the isolated outstation of Telefomin, near the West Irian border with Papua New Guinea. Two days later we walked into Telefomin, having camped along the way in a bush shack usually found in hamlets, and maintained for the use of Patrol Officers. The resident Patrol Officer lived in a bush material house near the air strip. There were no navigation aids or tower, just a faded wind sock at one end of the narrow unpaved strip. The officer helped with advice on our planned trek from hamlet to hamlet, traversing a circular route through the mountainous terrain.

We employed three carriers as guides and set off along the ridges and down steep gullies.

Patrol huts we used each night were about a day's walk apart. Our men were efficient fire makers, willing to show their skills using the twirling stick method. One man seemed to be awake all night to keep the fire alight. Also a stick to hold the door closed had the black billy attached, to fall and give warning of intruders. Now far from their home area, our guides were suspicious of their neighbours. One evening as driving rain swept across the steep slope along a ridge where lines of village houses clung, we were visited by a group of gourd wearing men who invited us to their spirit house. Their only covering, the 'Telefomin trousers', seemed to be such inadequate attire in the chilly 5,000 feet altitude. Men only were allowed inside the spirit house of bush material and bamboo walls. A ladder with cane lashed rungs led to an upper room where string bags containing soot-blackened skulls hung from the rafters. Ancestors with missing teeth formed an obstacle course for our heads. Pig jaw bones covered the walls, slotted into the bamboo weave.

We sat on the floor with these men whose long newspaper-rolled cigarettes added more fumes to the smoky, smouldering fire. A flat piece of tin contained the fire, which had a few sweet potatoes roasting in the embers. A young man who had worked on a copra plantation on the coast had learned Pidgin English. Pidgin is used throughout the country as a means of communication between the many tribes. It has been estimated that there are more than five hundred different dialects throughout Papua New Guinea.

Through the interpreter, we were able to converse with the older men, some of whom had never left their village and had not learned Pidgin. The rare encounter with the white visitors brought forth many questions from the men sitting around the fire. Our young interpreter kept the questions coming. Where had we come from? What were we doing in P.N.G.? Why visit this area? Hopefully our answers satisfied their endless curiosity. Without appearing too eager to leave the stifling windowless room, we thanked our hosts and descended to ground level. It had been a privilege to be allowed into this men's spirit house and a unique experience for all of us.

Barbara Gurney

Music Explosion

Crash - a cymbal strikes
    Quavers leap from the stave
        Attacks with frenzy
ebony and ivory assaults
    molests the mind
        dares recognition
trumpet and percussion
    reverberates through veins
        tells its story then settles
transporting melodies known
    with warmth and depth of tones
        a familiar blanket of joy
Sweet jewels of melodies linger
    transporting Vienna and maestros
        Violins and oboes
Rhythms soften to a heart-beating waltz
    Harmonies embrace
        Dance! It tells me

Rosemary

"Excuse me, are you in charge here?" A small voice interrupted Rosemary as she stood, tapping away on her iPad. She peered over the top but didn't see anyone. Must be going mad, she thought, shaking her head.

"Down here," the small voice called. She peered down and smiled.

"Yes, I'm in charge," she said. "My name's Rosemary and by the looks of your small stature, you're a new bank account pin number."

"Yes, that's right," the pin number replied.

"Well, OK then. Spit it out." Rosemary poised her finger above the iPad, ready to type.

"Spit what out? I'm not eating anything!" the pin number exclaimed.

"Your number! And please don't tell me you're 1234. We already have nine of those here." Rosemary rolled her eyes.

"No, actually I was supposed to be 5678, but he forgot to change me. So I'm still the original 9736," the pin number said proudly.

Rosemary tapped the number into the iPad. "So, where are your partners?" she asked.

"Partners? I arrived in the mail today. On my own. I don't have any partners," the pin number replied.

"Of course you do." Rosemary sighed. "All bank pin numbers are attached to a BSB and an account number." She looked at the newcomers that had just arrived. "You there—at the back. You look like a BSB. Do you belong to this pin number?" she asked, nodding in Pin Number's direction.

"I believe I do," BSB replied as he sidestepped the queue and walked forward. "I'm 036-001."

"Oh great. Another new one. He's gone and opened a Westpac account in the city now." Rosemary shook her head as she tapped away at the iPad. "You in the middle. Yes you, the big wide one. You look like a bank account number. Do you belong to these two?"

"I most certainly do," a loud voice replied. "I'm 0591137844987."

"Well, come forward and join your team," Rosemary said as she also entered the account number into her trusty iPad. "Now, the three of you must hold hands and make sure you always stick together. You need to move over there, to that section on the right, find an empty brain cell and jump inside."

"Eww, gross!" exclaimed Pin Number. "Are we in an actual brain?"

"That, my good friend, is the topic of many a debate. But in short, yes you are." replied Rosemary.

"Doesn't look like there are many empty brain cells left over there," said Account Number.

"Truth be told, I don't think there were many to start with." Rosemary smiled. "Now off you all go. As I said, stick together and DO NOT get mixed up with the others in the pin number group. Just sit in your brain cell and wait until you are required."

"How will we know when we're required?" asked BSB.

A large groan came from the Pin Number section.

"Oh trust me," said Rosemary, "you'll know. First of all, the brain cell you are residing in will start to constrict and it can be quite painful. Then if our host can't remember what you are, the pain becomes unbearable. He'll end up with a headache and of course, you'll get the blame. Now, off you go." Rosemary pointed them in the right direction.

After a couple of steps, they stopped. Pin Number turned around. "Rosemary," he said, "what are they?" Pin Number was pointing to the next group. "They look a bit, well, simple."

"They are indeed simple," sighed Rosemary. "They're called passwords. If you go and introduce yourselves, you'll meet ABC, XYZ and believe it or not, one called PASSWORD. There's even a really old one there called HARRY."

"Isn't Harry our host's name?" asked Pin Number.

"It surely is," replied Rosemary. "He's a hacker's dreamboat, our Harry."

"And that huge section over there?" asked Account Number.

"Well," said Rosemary, "that's the Facts and Figures section. It contains General Knowledge, Times Tables, that sort of thing. It's so large because we never throw anything out. Below that we have the Vocabulary section, with spelling and punctuation thrown in the mix. We even have a small section beyond that called the Foreign Language section. Although it's basically just old school boy French and a few Italian swear words. Now if you turn to the other side of the brain, you'll notice a sea of faces, all with tags hanging off their ears. They're all family, friends, neighbours or acquaintances and the tags show their names and where they are from. Unfortunately, sometimes the tags fall off and poor Harry gets a bit lost trying to remember a name when he sees a face. Below that we have two sections, Short Term Memory and Long Term Memory."

"Wow!" said Pin Number, "Why is Short Term Memory all covered in mist?"

"Mist? That's a light fog," said Rosemary. "Trust me, today's a good day. Some days it's a real pea-souper in there."

"What's that sound?" asked BSB.

"It's a song. From the music department down the bottom. Some days you won't hear any music at all. Some days you'll hear the same song over and over again. Depends on what Harry's heard on the radio."

"I don't recognize this song," said Account Number.

"It's 'Tie a Yellow Ribbon Round the Old Oak Tree'." Rosemary shuddered. "This one's been playing over and over for three days now. Personally I'd like to tie a yellow ribbon around old Harry's neck! Now, please go find an empty brain cell and settle in."

She turned to face some newcomers and started tapping on her iPad again. "Looks like there's a couple of new Italian swear words just arrived."

"Rosemary, before we go, what do you keep typing on that thing?" BSB was curious.

"Why, absolutely everything," Rosemary replied. "So I don't forget anything. I'm just Rosemary you know, a memory booster, a cognitive stimulant used to increase focus and memory retention. I'm not Wikipedia. At my age you don't expect me to remember everything, do you?"

Genevieve Leslie

Stars

Dark velvet blue
Ocean above
Storm the heavens
For a fountain of love

Thousands, maybe
Millions
Of diamonds
Shining in the night

I wish to see a place
That's far away
From here,
Where angels fly
And sweet birds sing

A place where I could
See you happy
And know for certain,
What we all wonder

A field to lay my dreams
Upon,
A dazzling, stunning
Place beyond reprieve

The safest place
Of hope and dreaming
Never-ending laughter
And light, ah such a sight!

Picture Hollywood
Filled with my favourite
People,
As Movie Stars gaze

We are all amazed
For no more wishful thinking
Living in a heavenly place
Lost days, memories erased
A heart fuelled only
By passion and love

Trip To Paris

As part of our holiday to the U.K., we decided to include a day tour of Paris. How exciting. The tour was fourteen hours (six am to eight pm), and included return tickets on the Eurostar, lunch at the Eiffel Tower, a river cruise on the Seine, and a coach tour of the city. We also had some free time to explore before our return journey.

We arrived at St Pancras International station in plenty of time; it was a hive of activity. We wondered why so many people were having breakfast in the cafes, as our ticket on the train included breakfast and dinner. At about five thirty am, we changed some money into Euros, then started looking for our tour guide. Some tours had a guide with a sign, waiting for their clients, but our tour had no obvious guide. We decided to go into the station complex, still no sign of a tour guide for our group. Being from Perth, we thought, No problem, all we have to do is find our carriage and seat on the train. We followed some people upstairs, and found a waiting train. We hurried along the platform, found our carriage, and sat down. A few minutes later, a man came along and told us we were sitting in his seat. The guard checked our tickets, and asked if we were going to Brussels.

We rushed off the train to find station guards looking for us. Just as well we had confirmed our trip the day before. At this late stage, we only had five minutes to spare. We raced up the platform to a waiting lift, ready to take us downstairs to another platform, where we were directed to our train. Another rush along a platform to find our carriage. We were finally in the right seats on the right train. About fifteen minutes into our journey, our tour guide finally showed up. She then told us our tickets were wrong, there was no breakfast or dinner included. Thankfully, the train had a buffet car, and we had some Euros.

As we approached Paris, it started to rain. Again, due to our naivety, we didn't bring an umbrella. We met our tour guide on the station platform, and she led us to our waiting coach, a ten-minute walk through the rain. The coach took us to a large shopping centre, where we had some free time to explore Paris. Of course, it was still raining, so we stayed inside the shopping centre. After meeting the tour guide again, our coach driver took us to the river for our Seine River tour. It was a bit cold and miserable, so we didn't see much.

At last it was time for our lunch at the Eiffel Tower. (Still raining.) Our friendly coach driver dropped us off close by, while our guide bought and collected our tickets. We didn't realise they were not pre-booked, so we had a long wait in a queue. There was no covered area, so we got very wet waiting for our disorganised guide. When we finally arrived at the restaurant, it was fantastic. The food was excellent, and the view spectacular, in spite of the rain. We tried to imagine how good it would look in sunny weather.

As we were finishing our lunch, our tour guide appeared again, to give us instructions for our coach tour. She pointed out our coach, which was parked down by the river. We had to walk down to the coach; she said there was no parking at the Eiffel Tower. Of course we wondered why the coach could bring us here, but not pick us up. The tour guide then disappeared, so we had no choice. We left with some others from our tour, and walked about ten minutes to find the coach, with everything (including us), looking wet and soggy.

I then struck a problem. We just spotted the coach when I fell down a set of steps. They looked flat to me, so I fell flat on my face. Luckily, my glasses flew off and weren't broken. I hurt my knees and grazed my hands, no serious damage. Someone helped me up, and I managed to get on the coach. The city tour was a blur to me, nursing my painful hands and knees.

Finally, we arrived back at the station, and the tour guide directed us to our seats. Of course, there was no dinner, so we arrived back in England tired, wet and hungry. As we left France, the rain stopped and the skies cleared.

My impression of Paris? A really beautiful city, maybe one day I will see it in the sunshine.

Valmay Bartlett

Writing on Subject

I made a wish
and my wish came true
I recount it now
as a warning to you

I wished for inspiration
and a colourful day
but when I awoke
the skies were still grey

My life is mundane
I have nothing to write
I decided to write nothing
and gave up the fight

I had to assemble
a doll's cot for my tot
the kit had five pieces
and that's not a lot

But each piece was attached
with a nail and a screw
so I brought out the toolbox
and read what to do

I don't know how I hammered
a nail into my thumb
it must have been something
incredibly dumb

The blood gushed out
a copious red
it made me faint
I bumped my head

I awoke this morning
with a leg purple and blue
I had a black eye
and my thumb oozed red goo

My wish came true
in such an unfortunate way
Oh why was the subject
a colourful day

Judi Priest

Learning to Forget
A Memoir

Saturday morning and I am up early. I'm going to a meeting out of town. What shall I wear? Definitely not that green top—it's getting a bit shabby. Hmm, the white top or the pink top? Either would be fine, I'll decide when I get dressed. Richard is coming around and then I will drive us—his health is fragile and he can't drive any distance. I've googled the address—need to turn right at the second roundabout coming into Hamilton (the church is on the left).

I jump in the shower, shave my legs, wash my hair. I'm going to a meeting— in Hamilton—turn right—turn left. The thoughts fly up and whirl about my head like scraps of paper. I try to catch hold of them but they slip through my fingers. When I catch hold of one it contains snatches of words and makes no sense to me—"meeting"—"turn right".

I am going—somewhere—where am I going? What am I doing?

I feel frightened and confused and I call out to my husband who comes to see what is wrong.

"Am I going to a meeting? Where is it?"

"You're going to a meeting in Hamilton."

"But I don't go to those meetings ... I don't know what I'm meant to be doing."

The tears are running down my face and my heart is beating fast. The scraps of paper are whirling faster and faster round my head and I can't catch hold of them. Doug looks worried.

"Can you dry yourself and get dressed? I'm just going to ring Richard then I'm taking you to the hospital."

"Yes." I know I can do these things. I dry myself ... I pick up my handbag ... I get in the car ... I see the front door of the emergency department at the hospital. Everything is disjointed and confusing.

"Am I meant to be going to a meeting? Where is it?"

The scraps of paper swirl faster about my head in a blizzard of white and I'm gone.

145

At the hospital they check my temperature (normal), pulse (fast) and blood pressure (200/90!). They ask me questions—What is your name? Do you know where you are? I know who I am and where I am and by all accounts I am pleasant and co-operative but very anxious.

"Am I meant to be going to a meeting? Where is it?"

Doug stays by my side while more tests are carried out and a brain scan is ordered. An orderly takes me to x-ray where I go through the scanner then I am taken back to ED where Doug is waiting. I know he is my lifeline and my anchor. He knows if I leave the cubicle I won't be able to find my way back. He answers my questions and watches me closely for any changes, tells me to rest.

"Am I meant to be going to a meeting? Where is it?"

"You were going to a meeting in Hamilton but you don't need to worry about that now."

Time goes by but not for me. I exist only in the present, in this moment, and in this moment, and in this moment and each moment once past is lost to me forever. I will remember nothing of these four hours.

Finally the white haze clears and the world comes into focus. I look around me. I am lying on a hospital bed in the Emergency Department of our local hospital. My husband and my sister are with me.

"What happened to me? How did I get here? I was going to a meeting."

"You were going to a meeting in Hamilton but then you weren't well. I brought you to the hospital."

"Did I dress myself?" I am wearing my old green top. Surely I didn't pick that?

My sister says, "Is she still going on about that bloody green top?"

Doug calls the doctor, tells him, "She seems different; something has changed."

The doctor is kind and patient. He asks me questions—my name, where I am, the date. I get the month right but not the day, but I'm only out by a couple of days.

He says, "I'm going to tell you three things and I want you to try and remember them. Book, table, horse."

He checks my pulse (normal), blood pressure (a bit high but lower than it has been since I arrived). He asks me if I know why I am at the hospital (I think Doug brought me but I don't know what happened. I think I was meant to be going to a meeting). He asks if I can tell him the three things he asked me to remember.

"Book, table, horse."

"That's right." He nods and smiles and Doug is nodding too. He looks tired but relieved. My head aches and the light hurts my eyes. I am very tired and I just want to sleep. My sister has gone to ring my parents and tell them I'm okay.

I stay in the hospital overnight while they monitor me to make sure there are no after effects. My doctor prescribes medication to lower my blood pressure and

I see the hospital neurologist. The diagnosis is Transient Global Amnesia—a form of migraine, unlikely to recur and with no lasting effects apart from having no memory of that four hour period.

Over the following days and weeks I will replay in my head the events of that morning. I remember everything from when I woke to the point where I called Doug to help me. I run my mental video player forward till the recording becomes patchy and crackled and only glimpses of the picture appear and then there is nothing—just a blank till I come round in hospital. Try as I might, I cannot find the missing four hours and I poke and prod at it for weeks until I finally accept that it is impossible to retrieve. For months I will worry if I forget something, lose my car keys, do something odd. I have to learn again how to forget. To accept that everyone forgets things and it is a normal part of how we function in our daily lives and not necessarily a sign of something sinister.

I have a second attack of Transient Global Amnesia. It's about two years after the first attack and I am at work. I feel it coming on and phone Doug to come and get me. When he arrives I am sitting in the tearoom with a workmate. She is preparing to call an ambulance. Doug takes me to hospital and again I lose about four hours. The diagnosis is quicker this time and when I come out of it I know not to try to recover the lost time. I try not to fight it and I let it slide away from me lightly so I can rest and recover. Dwelling on it doesn't help, only increases anxiety and prolongs the recovery period. The second time is not as traumatic and my recovery is quicker.

This time I see a second neurologist who carries out some standard memory tests. He asks me to tell him words starting with P and clicks a stopwatch. He makes tick marks on the page as I go through pen, panda, popular, patient, persistent. His eyebrows go up as I go through phantom, pharmacy and photograph and by the time I get to psychology, psychiatry and psychotic he has stopped ticking. He asks me to repeat strings of numbers—three digits, four digits, five, six, seven, eight.

"Accountant," says my husband wryly, by way of explanation.

The neurologist confirms that my memory is excellent and there is no cognitive impairment. I feel reassured and only slightly smug that I passed the tests. I think for a moment what it means to fail them.

I think sometimes what I experienced must be what it would be like to be in the early stages of Alzheimer's, but happening at a much faster rate. I remember the anxiety and stress of trying desperately to remember and failing. I remember how frightening it was. I learnt that when you are going through it, it helps to have someone with you who loves you to help anchor you to the world. And I learnt that forgetting is a part of living and sometimes it's important to let go and forget.

Genevieve Leslie

In the Top Cupboard

In the top cupboard
Is where I keep my
Favourite biscuits,
The ones with raspberry inside

In the top cupboard,
He leaves his keys
Spending hours looking for them
He returns, to find it there

It's the first place I look
To find my favourite mug
I'll make a cup of tea
You see, its doors are frayed
But it knows me

We keep our comfort food,
You know, when love
Is not ... in the mood
We go there, to feel better

He doesn't like to hide
Things from me,
I'd like to think, but
Sometimes — unpaid bills
Are found there

In the top cupboard
I leave my worries and cares
Locked away, safe
From troubling me
I'll come back to see them
Just as I left, unchanged

It's where I keep an extra
Box of tissues, for when
The tears find me,
And our little collection of coins
For our trip to the beach
When we need to just
Get away

Now I'd like to think, he'll always
Stay, but today
I heard the door close
He had left, before I could say ...
I opened the cupboard
To find a little box
With a beautiful ring,
In that moment
My heart began
To sing

Pat Marshall

Abbey

Abbey, little Abbey,
Abbey the butterfly girl,
Bright Catherine, strong like a diamond,
Abbey, a soft fragile pearl.
No one saw your anguish,
Nobody heard your pain,
Not even the lying monster
Who sought you again and again.

Catherine told her story,
Believable and true,
She even stated outright
That it had also happened to you!
She told it to so many people,
The police, her psychologist too,
The prosecutor, the Court, social workers,
Hoping they would know what to do.

Why did no one listen,
Take action to keep you safe?
You were let down by the system
Which kept him in your life.
He went to jail, but not for long.
Two years and he returned.
Abbey, all you wanted was for him to say sorry
Your forgiveness had to be earned.

Your friendship with Catherine
Was broken when she couldn't stay.
She had to start a fresh new life,
And so she moved away.
You must have missed her over the years,
The support she could have given;
On the few occasions you connected
It must have felt like heaven.

But the lies from him came thick and fast
When you had to see him,
Those access visits must have seemed like hell:
Why didn't you also accuse him?
No! Gentle Abbey couldn't escape
The contact, or the pressure
He kept up and increased
All the time in full measure.

He taunted you with the false tale
Catherine confessed her story was all lies.
He tried so hard to discredit her
In your unhappy eyes.
You would not believe him,
Defended her in your distress.
Your mother tried to help you,
But the situation was a mess.

The Court appointed "expert"
Must have seemed to be on "his" side.
The contact had to continue.
Was that when all hope died?
Or was it when you accused him,
After your memories came flooding back?
Of course he denied any wrong doing;
He claimed "white" when you stated "black".

Police Officers took your statement,
But "charges would not be laid".
It was always your word against his,

And so he never paid.
His position in the community
Was sacrosanct and firm —
His family, supporters from all over
Didn't know he was a worm.

The longer the contacts continued
The more distressed you became.
His continued denials depressed you
And so you turned to self-harm.
An eating disorder affected you
And other health problems arose,
Both physical and mental.
Not what a teenager would choose.

After school, friends came round;
Mother was there as well.
They'd laugh, and chat and argue,
As friends so often will.
You'd serve tea and cupcakes,
As a hostess should.
Such ordinary, normal, occasions.
Did they make you feel good?

Or did such simple activities
Bring anguish all the more
As a bruise, when you keep on prodding,
Just keeps on staying sore.
The healing balm you should have felt
From all those who were around you
Was blocked by so many unhappy thoughts
Which seemed always to confound you.

Tea and cupcakes in the afternoon
Were no celebration
But although a good experience,
It was no consolation
For all the happiness you had missed
When you were so much younger.

The misery and the anguish
Couldn't go on for much longer.

You retreated into your paintings and poetry,
And into your butterflies too.
All the time trying so hard
To work out what to do.
One last encounter with Catherine
Was still not quite enough
To stay your hand,
When things got really tough.

What were your thoughts on that last day?
Were they in a whirl?
The pain must have seemed unbearable
To such a sensitive girl.
Did you think Goodbyes to Mum and friends
And ponder what was to come?
A few last thoughts, then action:
And all the pain was gone!

Abbey, little Abbey,
Abbey the butterfly girl.
Abbey, little Abbey.
Crushed like a fragile pearl!

Never Again

It must never happen again;
That the rhythmic sound of wheels on the tracks
Instills fear instead of relaxation.
It must never happen again;
That fires glowing in the hearth
Instill horror instead of meditation.
It must never happen again;
That travel becomes a nightmare instead of a vacation.
It must never happen again;
That men become monsters instead of humanitarians.
It must never happen again,
It just must never happen.

Sioban Timmer

To Find Love ...

Find the one person
whose soul compliments yours —
Not someone to "complete you".

Find the one person
who can make your pulse race,
But whose heart beats in time to yours

Find the one person
who doesn't want you "perfect"
But is grateful for the imperfections that shape your being

Then you will find
A love that acknowledges who you were
A love that takes you as you are
A love that embraces the you—that you are yet to be.

Sue Palmer

Whispering Walls

"Disintegration, decay, disrepair, dilapidation, decrepitude, can't be me they are talking about," whispered the walls of the old ruins. "I may be showing a bit of wear and tear but I am not at the end of the road. There is a hive of activity going on in and around my walls.

There are so many visitors to these ruins and not all of them welcome. Take the historian for example, he's a very serious fellow who visits, studies my history, writes about my past, and he is methodical in his research. His documentation is so detailed. The archaeologist, he is the scientist who visits, he studies human history, and he is forever digging, digging, looking for human remains and artefacts. He is a little obsessive in his endeavours and should take greater care of my crumbling walls. Now the palaeontologist, this fellow studies forms of life existing in pre-historic or geologic times. He is looking for plants, animals and other life forms. I may be old, but pre-historic—I don't think so! I wish he would just move on.

The odd movie director visits, looking for the right setting for his latest movie. Various actors visit, they can be quite caustic in their comments. They just don't recognise the rustic beauty and character of old age when they see it. Then there's the ghost walks at night organised by the local tourist centre. I'm not comfortable with these strangers trudging through my grounds night after night. My walls are having enough trouble as it is.

The local children visit now and then, they love to climb, run, play hide and seek. I love the sound of their voices, I am reminded of distant voices now long gone. My current owners are caught in a battle with the local heritage council. The owners want to restore and build a home for themselves and their young family, but are meeting with opposition. It seems simple to me, funny that humans disagree over such matters, so I wait hoping for some attention and renovation.

Photographers see much beauty and are forever searching for just the right angle, mood, correct light and perfect moment. They want to capture colour, texture, the look of carved stone, soft, green moss growing on my weathered walls.

Artists spend long hours drawing and painting crumbling arches that were once doorways and windows. Birds and animals visit and burrow here and there. I like to think I provide a refuge for my friends. To witness a clutch of eggs in the nest, and know it won't be long until mum and dad will be busy feeding the new chicks, brings delight as I observe each cycle of life.

I am a romantic meeting place for young lovers. A secret place where words of love are whispered to one another, where plans are made to remain together, forever. And now we come to the last group of visitors. Some people come to take a look at me, walk around my deserted, unkempt grounds, weeds long overgrown. Others sit for a while, trying to catch a mood, a thought, sense an atmosphere, inspiration. They are welcome visitors, they are the writers. Writers of romance, mystery and intrigue, of murder, travel, fiction and non-fiction stories. Poets weave wonderful words as they create rhythm and rhyme to delight the reader. Others are gifted with the ability to write free verse, prose and short stories that draw the reader into worlds of times past and present. An appropriate title could be "Notes from the Old Ruins".

What stories are echoing around my walls? They could tell a tale or two, it takes time to pause and sit awhile. There are too many insistent voices that crowd creativity. So, come visit, stay for a time and listen, maybe you will find inspiration for your next piece of writing."

Carolyn Nelson

A Sad Awakening

I was sitting in the lounge room,
One of fifteen dinner guests,
The "odd-one-out" since Betty died,
At my first "sole" social test.
"Tom, you must come," Shelly begged me,
"Steve insists you do," she said,
"You can't turn into a hermit
Just because your wife is dead!"
She was not one to be tactful,
And I flinched at her cold words,
She and Steve; ideally suited ...
The same feathers for two birds.
Steve was known for being tactless,
I would just let it slip by,
But my Betty didn't like him ...
Though she never did say why.
It felt strange to be without her,
She would tease me ... "You're so blind,"
But I only saw my lovely ...
Betty filled my heart and mind.
Without her, to hold my focus,
I observed our friends at play,
I felt like an interloper,
Watching them behave that way.
"What on earth can Steve be thinking;
Kissing Willie Thompson's wife?"
I had whispered to my Betty,
"He could wreck his married life!"

157

Then I turned and spotted Willie
Kissing Shelly, in the hall,
Shocked ... I slowly came to wonder
If I knew our friends at all!!!
I stepped backwards though the French doors,
Hated feeling so alone,
As my old "rose-coloured glasses"
Smashed onto the paving stone.
My true love had made my whole life
Something beautiful and rare,
It had all become so ugly,
Since my Betty wasn't there.
Those who choose to play with fire,
Never think they will get burned,
And I thought of Sunday's sermon
On the wages sin had earned.
I went home and phoned our Sally,
Heard the smile in her sweet voice,
As she said, "Dad, please move closer,
Come to Broome ... you have that choice."
Should I stay with my memories?
Or move on to somewhere new?
I will have a chat with Betty...
She will know what's best to do.

Lynne Tatam

Reunion

You fled into the starry night
Quietly slipping away
Fifty years since losing the fight
It was not your time to stay

Fading memories are all that's left
In a world grown dark and cold
Lives shattered, hearts bereft
In sorrow I've grown so old

Your warm presence is very near
The air is strangely still
A ghostly smile dispels my fear
I exist but have no will

Eyes ablaze with infinite joy
A small hand holding mine
I see the man inside the boy
At last it is my time

Floating above this desolate place
We follow the North Star home
Your childish kisses upon my face
Never more shall I be alone

Life Is Not A Rehearsal

Childhood—carefree days of play. Kindergarten—wooden trucks and trains in a sand pit.

Then came real school and time took on a different meaning.

Tick tock

Hurrying up the street clutching a little cardboard case packed with vegemite sandwiches and granny apple for lunch. The assembly bell rings. Line up—march to classroom. Above the blackboard a large round wind-up clock shows hands moving, oh, so slowly.

Tick tock

Morning recess, more spelling, sums, writing. How much can a young mind absorb?

Time relentlessly marches on. Days into years.

Secondary school, serious study, homework overload, exams, reports. Ten years of learning.

Tick tock

But not finished yet. Five years of apprenticeship and night school.

However, it was not all work. Some social diversions were crammed into nights of badminton, weekends of tennis, beach, and picnics at Point Walter and Coogee with the gang on our bicycles.

Tick tock

Then came the motor scooter and the F J Holden. Freedom to join car treasure hunts and hang out at Bernie's Burger caravan on Mounts Bay Road. Can you smell the burnt onion?

Then came a break from day to day work. Across Australia by car with two school mates: destination Cairns. Overseas many years. Employed in six jobs on returning.

All good times; not a rehearsal but the real thing.

Tick tock

Index of Authors

www.ingramcontent.com/pod-product-compliance
Lightning Source LLC
Chambersburg PA
CBHW071252130626
46556CB00003B/1283